THE CORNER SHOP

Elizabeth Cadell

Chivers Press • Thorndike Press
Bath, England   Thorndike, Maine USA

This Large Print edition is published by Chivers Press, England, and by Thorndike Press, USA.

Published in 1997 in the U.K. by arrangement with the author's estate.

Published in 1997 in the U.S. by arrangement with Brandt & Brandt Literary Agents, Inc.

U.K. Hardcover ISBN 0–7540–3047–4 (Chivers Large Print)
U.S. Softcover   ISBN 0–7862–1195–4 (General Series Edition)

The text of this Large Print edition is unabridged.
Other aspects of the book may vary from the original edition.

Set in 16 pt. New Times Roman.

Printed in Great Britain on acid-free paper.

British Library Cataloguing in Publication Data available

Library of Congress Cataloging-in-Publication Data

Cadell, Elizabeth.
  The corner shop / by Elizabeth Cadell.
    p. cm.
  ISBN 0–7862–1195–4 (lg. print : sc)
  1. Large type books. I. Title.
[PR6005.A225C67 1997]
823′.914—dc21
                                 96–54261

CHAPTER ONE

The train was overcrowded when Mrs Abbey reached the platform. A nuisance, she thought irritably; she liked to arrive early and secure a corner seat—but nobody could have foreseen the long holdup of trains on the Piccadilly Line.

She was even later than she had realised; as she walked the length of the train seeking an empty seat, a whistle sounded and an official began banging doors. She darted to the nearest open one; a burly gentleman attempted to precede her into the compartment, but she had her own method of dealing with burly gentlemen who pushed; her capacious handbag, harmless when held under her arm, could in cases like this become a lethal weapon. One jab from the brass-bound end, and the gentleman, like all his pushing predecessors, gave way; as always, her quiet, deceptively mild air lulled the victim's suspicions and led him to conclude that it had been an accident.

There were no vacant seats, unless one counted as vacant the place over which an over-sized schoolboy stood guard while he hoisted his satchel on to the rack. A dig, and he had moved aside to rub his ribs; Mrs Abbey was seated. Even the schoolboy's fierce glare could not discover on her serene countenance

1

any consciousness of having usurped anybody's rights; this fact, added to his realisation that to demand a seat from a woman at least fifteen years older than himself would alienate the sympathy of the other occupants of the carriage, made him decide not to press his claim.

An hour and a half's journey. Mrs Abbey, with a resigned inward sigh, crossed her long, lovely legs and noted without interest the ensuing stir among her male fellow-passengers. She was aware that she was slim, blonde and beautiful—but her looks, though they might be alluring, were also misleading, and raised hopes which she was constantly constrained to crush. She had a clear brain, sound common sense and a capacity for hard work; why these sober attributes had been encased in so fancy a package, she had never been able to understand; she knew only that she looked far warmer than she felt.

At the end of fifteen or twenty minutes, she noticed that the train was slowing down; was there, she wondered, any chance of a corner seat? She glanced round the carriage. Yes, the woman over there was preparing to get out— and the stout man and the schoolboy were edging closer with a view to occupying the seat as soon as it was vacated. Well, she could deal with that. She glanced up at the rack as though looking for luggage, gathered her bag and newspaper, drew on her gloves and seemed about to alight. Before the train halted, she rose and moved to the door, allowing just enough room for the woman in the corner to get to her feet. The stout man and the schoolboy pressed forward—but they were too late; Mrs Abbey was seated, gazing out abstractedly at the fields bordering the station.

Now she was comfortable; now she could look through her notes. Ignoring the furious glances directed at her by the two disappointed candidates, she took out of her bag a sheaf of papers and gave them her whole attention.

It was irritating, she thought, to have been unable to put a finger on the trouble without coming all this way. Seldom was she forced to make a personal survey; her secretaries were articulate, experienced and reliable, and from their concise reports she was almost invariably able to deduce what, if anything, had gone wrong with any job in which she had placed them. But this post had been tried, and precipitately abandoned, by three of her most stable secretaries. Why? Miss Clarkson, perhaps, had been too young. Mrs Adamson— too old, too inflexible? But Olivia Bell was neither young nor old, and was noted for her skill in dealing with difficult employers—and even Olivia Bell had left at the end of the first day. Not one of the three, moreover, had seemed able to explain this uncharacteristic behaviour; in each case, the report had been far from clear, and the verbal complaints vague to the point of incoherence. It had been impossible to discover anything specifically wrong.

The advertisement—she studied it—had been straightforward enough.

Temporary resident secretary required by Professor to list contents of country house. Own cottage. Generous salary.

The Professor had cut it out of the newspaper in which it had appeared, and had sent it to her by post; he had explained that he had found nobody suitable among the applicants. Perhaps explained was hardly the word; what he had actually done was enclose the newspaper cutting with his card and a line written upon it: *Duds so far; have you anyone who would do?*

The Lucille Abbey Secretarial Agency, Lucille Abbey told herself with justifiable pride, always had someone who would do. In the six years since she had founded it, the agency had never lost a customer; believing passionately in giving value for money, she had also believed that for every employer, however difficult, there existed a competent secretary. Her success had stemmed from the success of her secretaries; satisfied clients had sent new clients and still more clients. An employer who had to leave her agency to go elsewhere would have meant not only a loss of prestige, but also the breaking of a proud record. *You want efficiency; we supply it* had been the firm's boast.

And this Professor had got through three of her secretaries in three days.

She looked at his card. Professor Hallam, Hill House, Holme, Hampshire; enough, she reflected, to make Eliza Doolittle swallow another marble. She had made the usual enquiries; he held the Charlesville Chair of Medicine at a famous university; his speciality was lungs. His father, an aged but still noted political historian, had died some years earlier while on a lecture tour in the United States, undertaken against the advice of his doctors. His mother had died in a London hotel only last month—which, presumably, was his reason for listing the contents of the house in the country. There had been nothing in his record or his background to arouse the slightest misgivings—so how to account for the reports of the secretaries? Take Miss Clarkson:

Job ill-defined. Cottage impossible.
Professor peculiar.

And Mrs Adamson:

No transport, no staff, no amenities.
Job impossible. Professor impossible.

And finally, the super-efficient Olivia Bell:

5

Regret unable to cope with job—or with Professor.

That last admission was, perhaps, the most baffling of all. It was taken for granted that the secretaries could cope with any type of employer; they could deal with, discourage or even disable the more troublesome ones. Peculiar? Miss Clarkson had been unable to amplify. Olivia Bell had said nothing. Mrs Adamson—deadpan Adamson—had come into the office on her return with what the receptionist described as a wild look.

Well, the mystery would soon be cleared up. After interviewing the Professor, she would catch the seven-twenty back from Strome Junction to London. She would have dinner on the train and be home in time to see the news and to finish her packing for tomorrow's journey to Paris. This was a waste of a nice, sunny September day—the first warm day for weeks. It was also a day robbed from her annual holiday, but it was worth it to keep ahead of her competitors.

She had not told anybody at the office that she was paying a visit to the Professor; it would have indicated dissatisfaction, and she had, as yet, no cause to lay any blame on her staff. She had taken leave of them and left them with the belief that she was leaving at once for her holiday.

If you could call it a holiday, she mused. A change of scene, of language, of job—but not exactly a rest. This would be the tenth year; perhaps the thing had gone on long enough; perhaps it was time to tell her aunt that after this year, she must find somebody else to look after the shop; she would like to see more of the world than Paris. But it was as well to remember that when she had agreed to her aunt's proposition, ten years ago, she had been glad enough to have two weeks' free accommodation, and her fare paid.

One problem at a time was enough; when the Professor was disposed of, she would think of Paris.

A steward went by, pausing at each carriage to announce that morning coffee was being served in the dining-car. It would be unwise, Lucille thought, to leave her seat; perhaps coffee could be brought to her. Signalling to the steward as he was on his return journey, she employed her smile as she had for other purposes used the brass end of her handbag—and with equal success; yes, the man said, he would make an exception in her case, and bring her coffee.

Half an hour, twenty minutes more. Gazing out at the endless procession of fields, fresh and green and glowing on this brilliant day, she experienced the feeling of loss of identity that always gripped her when she left London. She had been born, brought up, educated in

7

London; she had, she remembered a little hazily, been married there—her one mistake, now happily a distant memory. If she thought about her marriage at all, it was merely to confirm the wisdom of retaining the married prefix while reverting to her maiden name. The plan of opening an agency had already been in her mind, and she had decided that in business, Mrs. might carry slightly more weight than Miss.

The train slowed down; this must be Strome, the junction from which she would take the connecting bus to the village of Holme. It would leave in twenty minutes; there was time for her to get a drink of some kind, and some sandwiches for her lunch.

But Strome Junction, she found to her annoyance, was unlike any other junction she had seen; it was for trains only. There was a complicated system of lines, a signal box, three platforms with dilapidated waiting-rooms, rows of empty poultry boxes and, on all sides, interminably-stretching green fields. There were no houses in sight; apart from the signalman, looking out at her with obvious pleasure, there was no sign of life anywhere. She might, she thought angrily, have been abandoned in the heart of Texas.

From a waiting-room shuffled a down-at-heel porter, wiping his mouth and reminding her that she was hungry—and thirsty. No, he said in reply to her enquiry, there wasn't a

8

buffet. No, no bar. Milk machine? Out of order; had been since Christmas. Something to eat? Not on the premises, so to speak; he always brought his dinner, and he'd just eaten it.

Ten more minutes to wait before the bus took her to Holme. Every village had a shop of some kind; she would be able to get something to eat.

She walked to the small wooden bus shelter on the roadside. She sat on a narrow wooden seat and waited. After waiting for half an hour, she went back to the station to make further enquiries. Bus? Along any time now. Connection, it was. Never known it to fail, except now and then in bad weather, or when it broke down, or if the drivers got mixed up in their turns.

Going back to the road, she reflected without surprise on the local lack, the total lack of anything approaching efficiency. Once you got away from London, this was the sort of thing you could expect. It explained why she, and several million others, elected to stay in town. The outlook wasn't so bright, but the people were brighter. Things moved. People moved. And you could get a meal when you needed one.

The time dragged by. Trains thundered through the junction, or halted briefly before hurrying their passengers back to civilisation. She noted that nobody got out; what was there to get out for?

The unexpected check, however, had taken her mind off the Professor and directed it towards a more pressing problem.

To remarry ... or not?

The advantages were all too clear. Malcolm Donne was the only man she had met in the past few years who measured up to her standards for a second husband. He was forty, and a bachelor; he came from an old Scottish Catholic family. As well as inheriting more money than she felt anybody could reasonably need, he was a successful stockbroker. Like herself, he had come reluctantly to the idea of marriage; she had watched him overcome, one by one, his religious scruples and his social prejudices—he had good reason to fear that she would not fit into his somewhat staid, ordered, traditional way of life. He had a flat in London, but he spent his weekends, and most holidays, with his mother in Sussex, in the cottage built on three acres she had retained when the family estate had been sold. Here he indulged his love of country life and exercised his talent for organisation; he ran, or helped to run every activity in the neighbourhood. As the majority of these were concerned with outdoor sports, he found Lucille unable or unwilling to share his interest in them—she loathed what she called field-and-track events. Handsome as he looked in hunting pink, she saw no reason to squelch about in muddy lanes attending meets and cowering in hedges as the horses cantered by. Tramping round moors she considered a crazy proceeding. Point-to-points were the worst of all, with booted horsewomen expecting her to follow every event, and Malcolm alert to see that she did not shut herself into the car with the sandwiches and the sherry. Perhaps, married to him, she could make the children an excuse for staying at home—she knew that her chief reason for marrying him was to have a family.

It might be a cold-blooded approach to marriage, she mused, staring out over the fields bordering the rutted, empty road. But she had tried the other way, and it had led nowhere. There might be little passion in her feeling for Malcolm, but there was respect and a genuine fondness. They would have a beautiful home and their children would lead a life very different from the one she had led. They would have regular schooling, the attention of their parents, and a planned future. They would have a garden, and dogs; they would go abroad, not to stay with selfish aunts, but to enjoy themselves, and to see the world.

He had asked her to marry him and she had accepted—but after so much hesitation that he was uneasy. There was as yet no engagement, but he had decided to go over to Paris while she was there, and she knew that he would press for an early marriage and an immediate announcement.

With an effort, she brought her mind back to the Professor. Glancing at her watch, she saw that she had waited a full hour for the bus. It was half past two.

She heard a hoarse summons, and turned to see the porter making signs; she could guess, as she walked towards him, what he was going to say. She was right: the bus had broken down. Anybody waiting at the junction—clearly an unlikely possibility—was advised to take the three o'clock train, which would stop at Holme.

The three o'clock train did not thunder in; it jerked itself along as though every puff would be its last. It had only three carriages; the first was occupied by a placid-looking mother with a baby at the breast and two scarcely older swinging from the luggage racks. The next carriage was out of use, its upholstery having been removed—by vandals or for renewal Lucille neither knew nor cared. In the third carriage were two men, unwashed and unshaven and lying outstretched, fast asleep, upon the seats. She contemplated using her handbag technique to dislodge them, and decided against it; she would prefer, she thought, the company of the mother-of-three.

The journey took an hour. The train was a village-to-village one and stopped every ten minutes. People got in and got out, but in spite of her prayers, the mother and the three children remained. The two elder ones clambered on to her lap, opened her handbag to examine its contents, listened to her watch ticking, tried on her gloves, tore her newspaper, stumbled over her in fierce quarrels, ate oranges and bananas and dropped the peel at her feet. With the windows up, the carriage became a furnace; if she lowered them, dust and soot poured in and the children did their best to fall out. She alighted at Holme feeling as though she had taken part in a battle.

Holme. A platform, a straggling row of houses, a dusty-looking general store and—her eyes rested on it in horror and disbelief—a water pump. For the rest, rolling hills, with a distant farm or two to vary the monotony.

Enquiring about transport due to Hill House, she was told that a bus ran twice a day; it was due now, and it would take her most of the way. Almost at once, the bus came into sight; it slowed down, the driver leaned out, threw three parcels into the arms of a waiting porter, and drove on.

Lucille walked. The sun, which throughout August had shown no sign of existing, blazed fiercely, beating down on the unshaded road. Her hair clung damply round her forehead; her blouse became glued to her perspiring form. In the fields to left and right of her were great trees throwing patches of shade like dark skirts round their feet—but on the road there was only dust below and the flaming sun above.

13

She paused after a while and looked about her. She had been told that the distance was two miles—how far was two miles? She had no idea—but so far, the going had at least been level; now she saw, to her dismay, that the road was beginning to wind round the foot of a cone-shaped hill. Narrow and stony, it disappeared round one bend only to reappear higher up—and higher and yet higher. At the top of the cone, at what seemed to her an incredible distance, she saw a large, square house. Unscreened by trees, unsoftened by any gateway or drive, it looked down starkly upon the deserted landscape.

Hill House. Professor Hallam's house. If she still wanted him, there he was; all she had to do was walk up—or crawl up.

Close beside her she saw a path. Instead of winding round the hill, it went straight up it—a method that she, who liked direct approaches, could approve. It was steeper, but it was shorter. She took it.

Fifteen minutes later, she had lost all desire to interview the Professor. She had forgotten the points she had been going to raise regarding the scope of the work. Her plan of inspecting the accommodation seemed a fantastic kind of joke. The Professor's application should not have been made to her, she thought dully; she could supply efficient secretaries; she could not supply mountain goats.

14

She contemplated going back; she might as well give in; give up. But if she could only reach the house, she could sit down, cool down; she would be offered tea and she would ask for some form of transport for her journey down the hill.

She went on; soon, looking down, she saw a group of farm buildings. If she had come by the road instead of by the path, she would have passed close to the farm; she would have been able to ask for a lift to the Professor's house.

She stumbled, and saw that the heel of one of her shoes had come off; the other was loose; savagely, she tore it off. Then she went slowly, doggedly on to the top of the hill. She halted, panting, and blessed the breeze that had met her and was lifting her damp, lank hair. With coolness came a return of her accustomed calm; looking about her, she took stock of her surroundings.

She was standing at the edge of what at some time—before it slid down the hillside—must have been a garden. There were weed-choked paths, overgrown flowerbeds and half a rose garden—the other half had vanished in the landslide. Some distance away from her was a flight of steps leading to a terrace which appeared to run round three sides of the house.

She walked up and stood on the moss-covered flag-stones; then she approached the wide, oak front door. There was no bell and no knocker; her taps on the panels of the door

15

bringing no response, she decided to walk round to the other side of the house. She was going towards the corner when something made her pause. Built close to the house, so close that at first she mistook it for a summerhouse, was a small cottage. It was not more than twenty yards from her, across a weed-tangled drive, and its door stood open. She stood gazing at it, and rage slowly filled her.

Own cottage...

She went inside. There was one room with bare boards; through a half-opened door she caught a glimpse of a peeling bathtub. A huge, blackened stove, two wooden chairs, a heavy round table and, in the corner against a diamond-paned window, an enormous, brass-railed bed. A row of saucepans, a ten-gallon kettle, a sink with a single rusty tap.

Cottage? This ... this hovel? This, offered to a civilised woman?

Fatigue forgotten, she marched round the terrace. Wait till she saw this Professor. Only wait until she laid eyes on him.

She turned a corner and came to a stop. Before her was a man she identified unhesitatingly as Professor Hallam. He was bending over a glass-topped table, carving a cold roast chicken. Surrounding the chicken were several stacks of papers, two heavy books with knives placed in them as book-markers, three pens, a bowl of salad, a loaf of bread, a

16

glass jug full of milk, a panama hat with a battered crown, a dish of steaming potatoes boiled in their skins, a large roll of butter on a saucer, salt, pepper, oil and vinegar, a pair of socks and a paper bag spilling tomatoes.

The Professor placed a leg of chicken on a plate and bent to study a passage in one of the books. He was quite unlike the popular conception of a learned man. He was about forty, tall, clean-shaven, thin and wiry-looking. He wore large, round spectacles and had a very long, very straight, very sharp nose. He was dressed in crumpled corduroy trousers and a creased, open-necked shirt.

He picked up the jug of milk; Lucille saw his nose turning this way and that as he looked for a glass—like an animal picking up scent, she thought. He found no glass; placing the jug to his lips, he drank. As he lowered the jug, he caught sight of Lucille, and stood staring at her in astonishment, his mouth open, his upper lip decorated with a milk moustache. He was not peculiar or impossible, she decided; he was merely repulsive.

He straightened his spectacles as if to ensure that he had everything in focus.

'Not another secretary?' he enquired irritably. 'They come and they go. I asked for one, and three came. And went. You're the fourth. That agency—I don't for the moment recall the name—hasn't the kind of person I was looking for.'

17

His voice was crisp and authoritative and far from friendly.

'I came—' she began.

'Quite so. I'm sorry you had this trouble for nothing, but I told the last young lady quite distinctly that I required no more applicants. I have decided that I can manage better by myself.'

'Professor Hallam—'

'Yes, that's right. But I'm afraid you wouldn't suit me; you're not the type. For one thing, you're decorative, and while that wouldn't distract me, it probably distracts you. I would have telephoned to that woman to tell her she had completely misread my advertisement, but there's no telephone here. Thank you for coming.' He fumbled in a pocket. 'The expenses of your journey ... What do I owe you?'

She gave him a cold stare.

'Before we talk of expenses,' she said, 'may I ask if that ... that cottage is the one you intended to offer to the secretary you engaged?'

'Cottage?'

'Your advertisement plainly stated—'

'Oh, cottage; yes, now I follow you. Yes, I was quite prepared to offer it to a successful applicant, but as I've just told you—more than once, I fancy—I found nobody who suited me.'

'But you actually imagined that a secretary would inhabit that ... that hovel?'

' "Actually imagined ... actually imagined" '

He muttered the words with distaste. 'Extraordinary how the language is misused. One of those young women—the second, I think; no, the third—told me that the whole set-up was primitive. I'm quoting her own words. What she meant was that she was unable to light a stove or cook herself a simple meal.'

'On that stove in the cottage?'

'Exactly. Will you excuse me if I go on with my lunch? I became absorbed in some work this morning, and didn't look at the time.' He waved towards a basket chair. 'Please sit down; I can see that you have something you wish to say before you leave, but you must forgive me if I go on eating.'

She sat down. The Professor helped himself to potatoes, breaking them open and spreading butter liberally upon then. He mixed oil and vinegar with a crushed clove of garlic and poured the mixture over the salad. Turning the leaves tenderly, he glanced up at Lucille.

'You were saying?'

'I was saying the same thing as the third secretary said: the whole set-up is primitive.'

'Why primitive?' the Professor enquired through a mouthful of food.

'Obsolete. If you showed that cottage to the local authorities, they'd condemn it.'

'Condemn it?' The Professor picked up the chicken leg and bit off a piece of juicy flesh. 'Why on earth would they condemn it? It's

19

wind- and water-proof; it's sound, and it isn't even damp.'

'It isn't a place you could dream of offering a woman used to modern conveniences.'

'Ah.' The Professor hacked off several thick slices of bread and buttered them. 'What you mean is that those young women—and you too, I can see that—are unable to do anything for themselves. They were all at pains to state that they were educated women. Now, educated—would you very kindly pass me the tomatoes? Thank you—educated—look it up, if you like—means the strengthening of the powers of the body or the mind. To educate is to teach, to train, to cultivate any power.' He waved the chicken leg. 'Note that *any*. If a woman doesn't know that a match applied to wood makes a fire; if she can't understand that a fire boils water and boiling water cooks eggs, where is her claim to education? Where, if it comes to that, is her claim to being a woman?'

'Are you aware,' she asked furiously, 'that the term resident is taken to mean that meals and service will be provided? A resident secretary is a resident secretary; she is not a cook and she is not a water-carrier.'

'So numbers one, two and three informed me before they left. If secretaries are not resident, they go back after their work to something called a bed-sitter. Isn't that so?'

'Sometimes.'

'Where they cook eggs on a gas ring?'

'They've worked hard all day. Let me tell you that not one of my secretaries would dream of living in that cottage.'

'So before employing a resident secretary, I must employ a cook and a butler? Why,' he demanded, 'do you call them your secretaries?'

'Because they work for me. They're on my agency list. They are all competent—'

'You're the agency?'

'I am.'

'Do you mean you're Mrs ... whatever it is?'

'I'm Mrs Abbey; yes.'

'Why have you come yourself? Have you run out of so-called competent secretaries?'

'No, I haven't. I've run out of patience, that's all. I sent you three women whose records show that they had no difficulty in holding down any kind of secretarial job; after less than one day with you, they left. I came to find out why.'

'You've found out why, but if you're still in doubt, I'll tell you why they didn't stay: it was because, however impressive their previous records may have been, they couldn't do this job. The cottage you find so primitive is the remains of a seventeenth-century chapel; the original beams, the rafters untouched, those diamond panes full of beauty. The bed is well-sprung. There is nothing to dust, and only one floor to sweep. Wood for the stove is chopped and placed ready by me. Light the stove, make the bed, sweep the floor, heat some water—do

21

women really find that too much to undertake? How long did it take me to produce the meal I'm just finishing? Chicken sent ready to eat from the farm. Milk, butter and eggs, cream—would you kindly pass it? Thank you—also from the farm. Potatoes from the farm; I boil them in their skins and the entire process takes less than half an hour. Bread, also from the farm—home-made. Fruit from the farm. Stores are ordered and arrive every day. I think that if your three secretaries had paused to look into conditions, they would not have found them too primitive.'

He stopped; she said nothing. She sat silent, filled with rage and loathing—loathing of his level, precise tones, his unruffled manner, his long nose, his greed, his lack of consideration. She had nothing to say; she wanted only to get away from him, from the big, neglected-looking house, from the weeds and the nettles and the wide, empty view. Fumblingly, she gathered her bag, her gloves. She heard his tone of relief.

'Goodbye. I am sure you would not have been suitable; you have a tendency to carp. I—'

He came to an abrupt stop. Adjusting his glasses, he peered incredulously at her. He took them off, held them to the light, put them on again, gazed at her and spoke slowly.

'Are you *crying*?'

'Yes, I am,' she sobbed savagely.

'The fact that I mentioned carping—'

'If you were human,' she shouted furiously, 'you would have known that on a hot day people like to be offered a cup of tea. If you'd had one spark of consideration, you would have asked me whether I wanted to share your beastly chicken from the farm, and cream and butter and potatoes boiled in their skins in less than half an hour, instead of sitting there eating your head off and giving me lectures on education. You would have—'

'Look out!' He saved the milk jug from being swept off the table by her angry gestures. She rose, shame added to her miseries.

'Sit down,' the Professor ordered.

She sat down.

'Was that outburst of yours meant to indicate that you were hungry?' he demanded.

'I didn't have breakfast, because I never do, and I didn't have lunch.'

'Why not?'

'Because I counted on being able to get sandwiches at the junction.'

'Couldn't you have asked me for a share of my meal?'

'Couldn't you have offered it?'

'You arrived,' he pointed out, 'at ten minutes past four. I presumed that you had already had lunch, so I ate mine. It didn't occur to me that you might want tea. I'll bring you a plate.'

He brought one; she piled food on to it. He went indoors again, to return at length with a tray on which were cups and saucers and a huge brown earthenware pot of tea. He poured out a cup and placed it before her.

'Drink that,' he said. 'You look as though you need it.'

She sipped it, watching him put four heaped teaspoons of sugar into his own cup. He stirred his tea—clockwise, she noted, as her father had always done.

She did not speak until she had eaten and drunk. He sat gazing over the view spread at their feet. From where they sat, the ground sloped gently and then levelled out before the low hedge that marked the end of the property—and the edge of the hill.

'When was the landslide?' she asked.

He turned to face her.

'It happened when I was about six. I can still remember the fuss. My grandfather had been warned about building anything at that end, but my grandmother insisted on putting up a thing she called a Greek temple. That went, with the gardens surrounding it. A good thing, too; it blocked the best view of all.' He nodded towards it. 'Beautiful, don't you think so?'

'Yes. But if you're city-bred, you're city-bred.'

'And you are?'

'Born in Hampstead, school in Hammersmith, commercial school in Regent Street. Why did you need a secretary to draw up an inventory?'

'I didn't. I needed a secretary to type some papers.'

'Then why—'

'It was difficult to state baldly exactly what my needs were. I imagined that once I got hold of an intelligent woman, she would be able to grasp what was wanted. It was simple enough when I came here; all I thought I would have to do was draw up a list of the contents of the house, arrange for an auction, and go back to my work at the University. But in my father's study, mixed up with my mother's dress patterns, I came across some papers that my father had apparently been working on before he died. The reason I'd overlooked them when I went through his papers after his death was because my mother had done some clearing up before I got here; one can only be thankful that she didn't destroy the notes. Once I read them I realised their value, but before publishing them I had to sort them, transcribe them. It was work that seemed to me infinitely more valuable than drawing up lists of household effects—so I advertised for help. A secretary, I thought, could type the notes I got ready, and—in her free time—draw up lists of the contents of the house.'

'Why couldn't you have called in a valuer?'

'Because there was so little of value. Most of the furniture is run-of-the-mill, but my grandmother was a collector, in a mild way, and among the ordinary stuff there are some

25

good pieces. My mother travelled a good deal; most of the things she brought back were without value, but some of the ornaments are worth a good deal. So you see my problems: an intelligent woman—'

'—who would type difficult notes, light stoves, cook and clean, and who—'

'—who knew something about furniture; who could distinguish between turned taper and early cabriole, and recognise French scroll and spade. A woman who knew a rent table when she saw one—there's a good specimen in the house. But I shall be able to manage by myself. Nothing really matters but to clear up my father's papers and get his work into the publisher's hands. I've got three weeks or so free.'

She rose.

'Goodbye, Professor. Thank you for the lunch and the tea.'

'Goodbye, Miss Abbey.'

'Mrs.'

'Mrs Abbey. I suppose you came up in the cart?'

'What cart?'

He stared at her.

'Didn't you get a lift in the farm cart?'

'No.'

'Then how—'

She held out two objects. Peering, he recognised them as the heels of her shoes.

'You *walked* up?'

'I climbed up.'

'But I don't understand. The farm cart is always at Holme station to collect things off the bus—or to collect people.'

'One bus didn't run. The other didn't stop.'

He took the heels from her.

'Come with me,' he said. 'I'll mend them.'

He led her through the house, across a square hall, down a corridor and into an enormous kitchen; she had only time enough to glance at copper pots and pans, a scrubbed trestle table, a lighted stove, and then he was marching with long strides along another passage. He led her out into a very large yard surrounded by outbuildings; walking to one of these, he opened the door and ushered her inside. He handed her a pair of boots and held out his hand for the shoes.

She ignored the boots; perching herself on a stool, she watched him go to work. Absorbed in his task, he seemed indisposed to talk, but he answered, absently, the questions she put to him.

'When did your mother die?'

'A month ago, in London. I would have come down here earlier, but I was busy.'

'Did she live here alone?'

'She could hardly be said to live here at all; she liked moving about. There was a housekeeper here.'

'Why isn't she here now?'

'Because I didn't want her. She was an

27

irritating woman, and I wanted the place to myself.'

'Did she look after this great house all by herself?'

'By no means. She had helpers from the farm.'

'Did your grandfather build this house?'

'Yes. Like me, he was a lung specialist; he built it with the idea of running it as a sanatorium. Then he changed his mind, which was a pity. Good air, fine situation, and far too big for a family.'

She watched his hands; they were not workmen's hands, but they were deft and sure. The shoes mended, he sat contemplating them with satisfaction.

'There you are. Not a bad job.'

'Thank you.' She put on the shoes. 'And now, how do I get down the hill. How do *you* get down the hill?'

'I always ride.'

'Bicycle? Horse?'

'A mare. I ride her down the hill, and she waits for me at the farm. If I don't want her to wait, I send her up again. If you'd like to ride her, you're welcome to do so. Do you ride?'

She had, in childhood, ridden a donkey at the seaside. At school, she had several times scrambled upon a sleepy horse called Hector and, attached by a leading rein to the mount of the old lady who ran the local riding school, proceeded sedately along secluded bridle

28

paths. But Hector and the old lady had died, and with them, her ambition to be a horsewoman.

'Yes, I can ride,' she said. 'But I'd rather walk.'

'Nonsense. There's rain coming, and it's getting dark. You wouldn't be able to find your way in the dusk, unless I went with you.'

'I shall be perfectly all right,' she said.

'You've no mackintosh.'

'Yes, I have. A plastic one, in my bag.'

'Then put it on.'

He went out to the yard. He vanished into a stable and reappeared holding reins and a saddle. Filled with sudden apprehension, she hurried after him.

'I can't possibly ride in this skirt,' she pointed out.

'Tuck it up,' he directed.

He walked towards an archway and began making coaxing sounds. After a time, there came the noise of hooves; then an animal of what seemed to her gigantic proportions came through the archway and began to nuzzle the Professor's shoulder.

'When you get to the farm,' he instructed, throwing the saddle over the mare and adjusting the girths, 'tie up the reins and just give her a slap and send her back. She'll understand.'

Terror was creeping over Lucille, but she would have died rather than say so. Under the

29

Professor's impersonal gaze, she adjusted her skirt to give maximum freedom to her legs. There was nothing to worry about, she told herself firmly; you got up from the left-hand— what they called the off, or was it the near?— side. You took hold of the stirrup and turned as though you were going to start off in reverse, and then somebody gave you a heave and all you had to do was make sure you didn't go clean over.

She did not go over. Propelled by the Professor, she landed face-down on the mare's neck.

'Steady,' warned the Professor. 'Bit out of practice, aren't you?'

She struggled to a sitting position, and summoned pride to her aid. The Professor stepped aside.

'Goodbye,' he said.

The mare stood stock still. Lucille kicked with her newly-mended heels and made encouraging noises; then, desperate, she remembered that she had in her possession a weapon better than any heel-digs. With her handbag, she gave the mare a jab.

The next few moments were to remain always a blank in her memory. When she next took stock of her surroundings, she saw that she was descending, with sickening jolts, the steepest part of the hill. She clung to the mare's mane; her fingers felt permanently locked. Rain began to fall, and she remembered with dismay that the farm was by no means the end of her journey; there was still the village, the junction.

She could see the farm; as the mare approached it, the ground became more level and the animal broke into a spirited trot. Teeth clacking, every bone in her body jolted, Lucille strove in vain to achieve the rhythmic up-down, up-down which was so easy once you could do it.

The suddenness with which the mare halted gave her the greatest jolt of all. Almost thrown, she managed to regain her balance; all she had to do now, she thought with infinite relief, was to get both her legs on to the same side, and slide down.

She had no time to carry out this manoeuvre. The mare, perhaps puzzled by the undue delay in dismounting, perhaps eager to return to her master, perhaps unwilling to stand motionless in the now-pouring rain, turned and headed for home.

There was no question of getting off. Only a circus performer, or a Cossack, could get off an animal that was travelling as fast as this one.

The buttons had been torn off her mackintosh; her skirt was in shreds. Her plastic hood was somewhere on the hillside. Her hair hung limply about her face. Misery enveloped her, colder, more damping than the rain. Mist drifted down and closed about her; terror gripped her and held her.

31

The mare took the last part of the journey at a canter, and came to a halt so abrupt that she lurched forward to rest on its neck. Straightening, she saw before the archway through which she had ridden—how long ago, she could not imagine. From the kitchen door she saw the Professor approaching. He put a hand on the mare's bridle and then, peering through the mist, saw Lucille.

'Will you please,' she said in a shaking voice, 'get me off this animal?'

He lifted her down. It was not a graceful descent, but she was past caring.

'I'd like a torch,' she said with chattering teeth. 'N-nobody's ever going to get me on a h-horse again. I want a torch, please. I want to go home.' Her voice rose in a wail. 'I want to ... go ... home.'

Without a word, he took her arm and led her past the kitchen and into the cottage. She made no protest; exhaustion of a kind she had never felt before was closing in upon her; she knew enough to be aware that for the present she had done all she could do.

'Strip,' ordered the Professor. 'I'll get you something to put on.'

Something to put on was not only a woman's faded, old-fashioned dressing-gown, but also sheets and pillow-cases for the bed.

'You make the bed; I'll fix the fire,' he said.

He fixed it—even through her exhaustion, she was maddened by the ease and speed with which he performed the task. The wood crackled, a glow appeared, warmth began to pervade the room. The Professor swung a chair round with its back to the blaze.

'Hang your things on that,' he said.

He went out and closed the door; the puddles from her streaming garments spread and then began to steam. She undressed and wrapped herself in the dressing-gown—a tall woman, whoever she was or had been—and spread her wet clothes on the chair. She made up the bed, longing to climb between the sheets and close her eyes and open them in the morning not to a new world, but to the old one. Tomorrow she would go back to where she belonged.

She heard a shout; opening the door, she stood aside to admit the Professor, who was carrying a laden tray.

'Here,' he said, putting it on the table. 'Take that, and then get some sleep.'

He went out. There was no tray cloth. There was a plate on which were three thick slices of bread; there was butter on a saucer; three boiled eggs, and a mug filled with hot milk.

She left nothing; when she had finished, she carried the tray to the kitchen. She washed the plates and the cup at the vast sink, dried them on a cloth and was on her way back across to the cottage when she heard the Professor's voice. He was at an upper window—in process, she saw, of changing into dry garments. The rain had stopped; stars were beginning to show in the sky; the mist had disappeared.

'Look, Miss...'

'Mrs Abbey. It isn't a difficult name to remember.'

'Your skirt ... you won't be able to mend it before you go. I'll bring you one of my mother's.'

He brought it and dropped it on the bed.

'I work in the mornings,' he said. 'I'd be glad if you went away without disturbing me. Take what you like from the kitchen. I'm going into London tomorrow morning; I'll call in at the Agency and tell them not to send anybody else. I'm sorry you've had all this trouble for nothing.'

'Goodbye, Professor.'

'Goodbye, Miss...'

'MRS. ABBEY,' she yelled in fury.

She banged the door behind him with such force that the crash dislodged one of the diamond window-panes. From outside the door she could hear the Professor's angry comments; ignoring them, she got into bed, closed her eyes, decided that the mattress was made of a mixture of wool and hillside stones, and fell asleep.

CHAPTER TWO

She woke to see early morning light filtering through the window. Closing her eyes, she lay still, her mind glancing off yesterday and coming to rest thankfully on today. She felt rested and relaxed; the self-confidence that had deserted her the day before was restored.

She saw that it was only just after six. She remembered vaguely a brief waking interval during which she had thrust logs on to the fire and closed the window—the air coming through the missing pane was more than enough. The bed had been less comfortable than the Professor had claimed but, exhausted as she had been, she would have slept soundly on straw.

Burrowing her head into the pillow, she prepared to sleep again. She drifted for a time in a pleasant half-conscious conviction that she was in her own flat, back in London, back at her desk, her life proceeding as smoothly as it had done for the past few years. She had almost fallen asleep when she was roused by shrill cries outside the window.

'Butter and bacon?' screamed a high voice. 'Yeah, I got that, Professor. How 'bout eggs? An' Mum says wouldn't you like a nice duck? She's been keeping one for you.'

'No duck,' came from the Professor's voice

from an upper window.

'Aren't you tired of chickens?' asked a second voice, slightly lower but no less piercing than the first. 'There's a couple more we put in the kitchen. Chicken, chicken, always chicken; you'll soon be cheeping, Professor. What else, Roz?'

'Bread,' Roz replied. 'And apples. Ask him about the apples, Red.'

'We've got bread, and some nice juicy windfalls,' Red shouted. 'Shall we leave them, Professor?'

Unable to bear it any longer, Lucille threw back the covers, opened the window and looked out. She saw a boy of about fourteen— his hair left her in no doubt that this was Red— and a girl slightly younger. Both were stocky, freckled, snub-nosed and sharp-eyed; both wore blue jeans and checked shirts.

'Will you kindly continue this conversation somewhere else?' she demanded.

There was no reply; her appearance had left Roz and Red regarding her open-mouthed.

'It's only just half past six,' she pointed out. 'That's no time to shout outside people's bedrooms.'

Red found his voice.

'Professor,' he yelled excitedly, 'there's a lady down here.'

'A girl,' screamed Roz.

'In the cottage,' shouted Red.

'In bed,' supplied Roz.

36

Lucille glanced upward. The Professor was at his window, shaving, his gaze on a shaving mirror placed on the sill.

'She's about twenty,' Red said after a further survey of Lucille.

'Twenty-five,' corrected Roz.

'An' she's got blue cross eyes—I mean blue eyes that look cross. She's wearing a nightie.'

'A dressing-gown,' amended Roz.

'It looks like one of your old Mum's—I mean an old one of your Mum's, Professor. She—'

There was no point in continuing; the Professor had withdrawn, closing his window with a decisive bang. Lucille closed hers and went back to bed. She drew the sheets up to her chin and shut her eyes, but she knew from the whispering sounds outside the window that the pair had not gone away. In a few moments she heard herself addressed.

'Miss! Hey, Miss! Can we have a word with you?'

A brown eye—Roz's or Red's—was looking through the diamond aperture. Like the voice, it was full of pleading.

'Go away,' Lucille requested.

'Couldn't you just listen for one minute? Please, Miss. It's important; it's terribly important.'

'Will you please go away?'

The eye vanished. She heard some agitated muttering, and then footsteps retreating; Roz

37

shouted an invitation to Giddup, but it was not addressed to her; it was followed by the sound of hooves and wheels on the stony road. Relieved, Lucille drifted into sleep.

She awoke some time later to the sound of cautious knocking. When she answered, the door was pushed open; on the threshold, carrying a large, laden tray, she saw Roz. Behind her were two smaller girls bringing plates and a teapot.

'Thought you'd like your breakfast,' Roz said, putting the tray on to the table. 'I made tea, but if you'd like coffee, rather, I'll make it for you in a jiff.' She jerked her head towards the younger children. 'Those are my sisters, Al and Dot. Red wanted to come, but he couldn't because of you being in bed. He's waiting outside.'

Lucille looked, shuddering, at the tray. She saw two fried eggs, half a dozen curls of bacon, a thick slice of fried bread and two fried tomatoes. She closed her eyes and spoke faintly.

'It was very kind of you,' she said, 'but I only take tea—nothing more.'

'Told you so,' Red said from the doorway. 'Tea and toast was all she'd like, I said.'

'You get out,' Roz ordered. 'I told you you couldn't come into a lady's bedroom. Eat up, Miss.'

'It's very kind of you, but ... No. No, thank you.'

38

'But this isn't morning tea; it's breakfast,' pointed out Al.

'I'm afraid I never take breakfast.'

There was a pause.

'Mind if we eat it?' Dot asked delicately.

'I wish you would.' Lucille sat up. 'Just give me the tea.'

Roz poured out tea that was almost black, poured in milk until it brimmed over the side of the cup and, before Lucille could prevent it, three spoonfuls of sugar.

'There you are,' she said, carrying it to the bed. 'You drink that up. Then we'd like to talk to you.'

It was impossible to refuse the proffered cup. Lucille drank. Roz drew a chair up to the table and divided the food into four portions; she handed Red his share and then sat down to eat with Al and Dot.

'I suppose you're from the farm?' Lucille said.

'Yeah,' Roz nodded vigorously, the fat from the bread glistening round her mouth. 'Sorry Red and me woke you up so early. We come up every day before school, to see what the Professor wants to eat. After school, we bring the stuff. He orders the same every day, nearly; chicken, eggs, salad and that. Never changes. You'd think he'd get tired, wouldn't you?— What's your name, Miss?'

'Mrs Abbey.'

'Mrs!' The freckled face lengthened in

39

dismay; egg dripped halfway between mouth and plate. '*Mrs!* But if you're Mrs, then—'

'Use your brains, can't you?' Red shouted through the pane. 'If she came after a resident job, her husband must know, mustn't he? If he's around, that is. Maybe he died.'

'He didn't die,' said Lucille.

'Divorced,' Roz decided, relief in her voice. 'Then that's all right; you could stay if you wanted to. You get away from that window, Red. Mrs Abbey's going to dress. When you're dressed, can we talk to you, please?'

'What's the matter with talking now?' Lucille asked.

'Well, Red's the one to explain everything, and you're in bed.'

'I may be in bed, but as you can see, I'm draped in a large dressing-gown.'

'Yeah, but you're still in bed,' Roz said with a finality that closed the subject.

She carried the tray away and returned a moment later with hot water.

'We'll be outside, waiting,' she said.

Left to herself, Lucille dressed. Opening the door and stepping outside, she saw no sign of the children, but the beauty of the morning made her pause and gaze out at the wide, green landscape. Not only did it look lovely, she admitted, it smelt lovely too. Freshness and sharp, sweet, strong air and not a hint of diesel fumes. But not even a prospect like this, she thought, had half the attraction of her small

40

flat, her bright, busy office off Sloane Street with her name on the outer door and *Private* on her particular door.

She thought of Malcolm Donne, and her heart sank. She was not equipped for country life. She wanted pavements and intimate little restaurants that served salad lunches; she wanted libraries and laundrettes. She did not want to change her way of life, narrow and selfish though it might be. She had got where she was—many people would think it not very far—without money, without academic training, with only her good business sense and her natural ability to get on with and to manage women. Men had played little part in her life; until she met Malcolm, she had had no desire to remarry; love affairs she considered inconclusive, exhausting and far too heavily weighted in favour of the man.

She turned to look at the house. It was larger than she had thought; in the morning light it looked substantial and almost handsome.

She sat on a low, ruined balustrade and stared down the hillside. The mare, grazing close by, came nearer and, receiving no encouragement, went away again. The silence seemed to press on her; she could hear only bird calls and the occasional lowing of cattle. Some distance away she saw a cart, its horse freed and grazing beside it. This, she supposed, was what the children had come up in; what she should have come up in yesterday; what she

41

would certainly go down in today.

The thought of leaving brought less pleasure than she had expected, and once more, depression filled her mind and seemed to weigh her down. She would not be going home; she would be going to Paris. When she returned from Paris, it would be to a changed life.

She walked out of the shelter of the house, and the wind tore at her hair and lifted her borrowed skirt. Up here, she thought, it must blow most of the time. Facing it, feeling its coolness, she saw the children coming towards her.

She led them back to the cottage; they filed in after her, looking serious and purposeful; they placed a chair for her and stood round taking her in with frank, unabashed stares.

'I'd be glad to borrow that cart to go down the hill,' she said.

'That's what we want to talk about,' Red said soberly. 'Do you have to go?'

'I don't *have* to; I *want* to.'

He was clearly the spokesman; the others were content to leave matters to him.

'What we want to say is, why can't you stay? The others didn't but then they just came and went, straight off. You didn't; you stayed the night, so you must've liked it better than those others. So this morning early, when the Professor didn't order anything for you, we knew that unless we said something, you'd be going off.'

'Yes, I am. I'm sorry, Red; I'm going, just like all the others.'

'But why? You came after the job; why not give the Professor a chance? He's not as daft as you think; it's just that he's a bit different, that's all. It isn't his fault that the job took longer than he thought. You could stay and help him. And not only him—the French gentleman.'

'French gentleman?'

'Yeah. Four times, he's been here, but the Professor won't pay any attention. He won't even talk about the pictures.'

'What pictures?'

'The pictures that the Professor's mother painted. They're in the house, but that old housekeeper, Mrs Westover, locked up most of the rooms when she left, and so nobody but the Professor can get at the pictures—and he won't bother himself, because he says this work he's doing—his father's papers—is more important. Until that's done, he says, he's not going to stop for nobody.'

'And what did you imagine I could do about it?'

'You could help him to get through the work faster. You could help him sort, and type, and file, and all that. And once it was done, the French gentleman could buy the pictures. He's been hanging about and he's angry, because it's wasting his time and his time's valuable, he says.'

43

'Well, I've every sympathy for him,' Lucille began, 'but—'

She stopped; the children were not listening. They were at the door, peering out. Going to stand beside them, she at first saw nothing that could account for their breathless interest—then, at the bottom of the hill, about to begin the steep ascent, she saw a car.

'The French gentleman?' she hazarded.

'Yeah,' said Red. 'Didn't take long, did he?'

She fixed him with a cold look.

'Didn't take long to what?' she enquired.

Red's cheeks began to take on the colour of his hair.

'Well, he didn't take long to . . . to get here.'

'What did you do—telephone?'

'Well, I promised him,' muttered Red.

'Promised him what?'

'I said if a secretary came, I'd phone him. Some came, but nobody stayed, so I didn't phone. Only this morning.'

She said nothing more; there seemed no point in enquiring how much he was paid for his services. The Frenchman, she thought, must be astute; tackling the Professor must have been like knocking on granite, but he had managed to devise a method of keeping in touch.

The children seemed to feel that they had done their part; she watched them climb into the cart and drive away. Car and cart paused briefly as they passed one another; then the car

44

came on. She could make out details: it was chauffeur-driven; the passenger sat behind. As they came nearer, she saw that the chauffeur looked sulky—no wonder, she thought, if he was thinking of his tyres.

The car reached the level of the house and scrunched over the gravel path. It stopped, and the chauffeur went round to assist the passenger to alight.

After the Professor's casual, creased appearance, after the children's well-worn clothes and her own borrowed skirt, she could gaze with peculiar pleasure at the impeccable grooming of the visitor. From his well-brushed hair to his burnished shoes he carried her back to her familiar world—a world in which successful men carried on successful businesses. In his middle forties, he was also of middle height; he was slim and clean-shaven, with dark hair touched with grey, and eyes— large, velvety, long-lashed—that would have made any woman beautiful. She looked for a word that would sum him up, and thought that urbane might do.

He came up to her and gave a slight bow; she saw his smooth skin and, as he smiled, his strong white teeth. His nose was well-shaped, slightly arched; comparing it with the Professor's arrow-head, she found it impossible to believe that they could be the same organ.

'Mrs Abbey?'

'I've just learned that Red telephoned to you.'

He laughed.

'You're not angry?'

'No—but *you* should be; he's brought you all the way up here for nothing.'

He made no reply. He was looking round for a place in which they could shelter from the wind. He indicated the low bench outside the cottage; the chauffeur dusted it and went away. Lucille sat down and the Frenchman settled himself beside her.

'First,' he said, 'would you have the kindness to tell me your first name? You do not look like a Mrs Abbey.'

'Lucille.'

'Will you permit me to call you this?'

She nodded, lost in the pleasure that had filled her at the discovery that he sounded almost as attractive as he looked. His English was good, his accent slight; his voice was melodious, and he used his hands and shoulders freely. He was a charmer; practised, almost professional, but she had no objection to being charmed. A performance as artistic as this, she considered, was well worth watching.

'How much did my friend Red tell you?' he asked.

'You're a Frenchman, name unknown; you've been up here several times trying to direct the Professor's attention to some pictures you want to buy; the Professor refuses to show the slightest interest.'

'That is a good summary. Will you permit me to enlarge a little upon it?'

'Couldn't we just agree that I've made up my mind not to stay here? I didn't come to take the job in the first place; I merely came to see why none of my secretaries could stay with the Professor for more than a day.'

'Your secretaries?'

'I run the agency they came from. I came to see what was wrong with this Professor.'

'The customer is always wrong?'

'My secretaries are all ambitious—which means that they'll do anything they can to help or to humour their employers.'

He gave her a long scrutiny.

'And you, too—you are ambitious?'

'Up to a point.'

'Then is there any way in which I can bribe you?'

She laughed.

'No. What's so special,' she asked, 'about the Professor's mother's pictures?'

'According to the Professor, they are worthless—but in this matter, it is only his opinion that is worthless. Would I stay in England, hoping day after day to make the Professor see some reason, if I did not see some profit to be made?'

'I suppose not. But if the house and its contents are to be sold—'

'Ah, but my dear Lucille, you have not yet

47

heard how it is that I have come here. Will you listen while I tell you?'

She nodded, her eyes on the quiet hillside. From the house came no sound; one of the open windows on the ground floor would be, she supposed, that opening out of the Professor's study; he would be in there, working, forgetting to look at the time until his stomach cried out for potatoes in their jackets. Beside her, the Frenchman spoke in his low, pleasant voice.

'My name,' he said, 'is Paul Reynaud. There are many thousands of Paul Reynauds; it is like saying, in this country, I am John Smith. But the name—my name—stands in large letters outside three well-known galleries; small galleries, but famous: in Paris, in Rome, in Milan. One day in June, a lady came to my Paris gallery. She offered me some pictures. She—'

'The Professor's mother painted professionally?'

'No. She was an amateur. She was, shall we say, dedicated to art. She spent a great deal of time in France and in Italy and in Austria, painting, meeting artists, helping artists; if she admired an artist's work, she would become a patron or a pupil—even a disciple. I was interested in the pictures she showed me, but I was to leave immediately for Milan. I asked her to come back. She did not come back. She left no pictures, she left no address; I knew nothing

48

of her, and the artists who could speak of her did not know where she lived. But I had been interested in her work, and I was sorry to have missed the chance of buying it. The pictures I sell are good pictures, but they are something more: they are very often new pictures. My gift—perhaps I may be frank and claim that it is a great gift—is for knowing which pictures, often by unknown artists, are going to become known, become fashionable, increase greatly in value. It is these pictures, you understand, which bring me the most profit. I am willing to bid for Mrs Hallam's pictures wherever they are on sale, but as she came to me in the first place, it seemed to me that I was justified in seeking her out and coming to terms with her.'

'How did you find her?'

'By the merest chance. I saw her name—Hallam—in an English newspaper. Two lines. There had died, it said, the widow of the famous political historian, Claud Hallam. It did not give her full address, but it was enough. I came here. And then?'

'The Professor was busy.'

'Yes. He told me, and in a way far from polite. Do not think that I cannot estimate the value of the papers he is working on. His father was the greatest living authority on—'

'Yes, I know.'

'You have read about him?'

'No.'

'Then—'

49

'I know all about greatest living authorities. I know all about professors and their papers, too. I'm the greatest living authority on what it's like to live with a greatest living authority. It's an art; a difficult art. It's a privilege too, of course—but I was only twelve when my mother died, and I was too busy from then on to understand just how great a privilege it was. If you hope that by persuading me to stay here, you'll get those pictures any more quickly, you're going to be disappointed. Where men like the Professor are concerned, nobody can help you. I know, because I lived with one. My father went upstairs to his study every morning and stayed there all day, lost to the world and to humdrum little details like food or clothing or school bills or tradesmen's accounts. Nothing existed for him but the work he was engaged on. Nothing exists for this Professor but the work he's engaged on. The only advice I can give you is to go in there and take a look at the pictures and—'

'Ah! But then there is a further complication. The pictures are locked up. And it is in this that you can help me; it is for this that I beg you to stay. You see, Lucille, it seems that when Mrs Hallam was alive, a house-keeper looked after this house. When Mrs Hallam died—this I have been told by the mother of Red—the house-keeper wished to stay on. She wrote to the Professor to propose this. No, he said; I no longer need a house-

50

keeper, because the house is to be sold; please to close up all the rooms except the bedroom and the study and the kitchen and the bathroom. So she did this. She closed and she also locked up all the rooms not to be needed—and then she went away. She was old, and they say incompetent; she labelled nothing, and she did not separate the keys in use from the keys not in use; they are there, jumbled up, waiting for the Professor, or for somebody else, to unjumble them. If you stayed, everything would be arranged: you would help the Professor with his papers, and in this way he would finish them quickly; you would begin to make lists of the furniture—is this not the work for which he needed a secretary? You would ask for the keys, you would open the doors, and then I could buy the pictures from this crazy Professor. I will go on my knees to him; I will not bargain; I will say "give them to me at whatever price you name, and I and my chauffeur will carry them away with no trouble to yourself." Is this too much to ask?'

He stopped. Taking out a handkerchief, he wiped his brow.

'I am stupid. I get too excited,' he said. 'But to be held back, held up in this way, without good reason—that is enough to anger a man, don't you agree?'

She did not answer, for she had not heard the question. She had not been listening; she had ceased, for the moment, to think of Monsieur

Reynaud or the Professor or the problem of the pictures. She was thinking of the future; her mind was on herself.

Her way of life, she knew, was about to change. She would marry Malcolm Donne and become the mother of his children and live on a farm and become familiar with cows and bulls and hounds and horses. As lives went, it would be a good one; she was lucky and she ought to be feeling thankful and happy.

But she was feeling far from happy. Events seemed to her to have moved too fast; she was not ready to make the final, the irrevocable decision. And here, at hand, was a means of putting off, for a short while, the move from the pleasant present to the unknown future. Here was an opportunity of pausing on the brink; of getting away, of losing herself, of drawing back to take a last detached look at life. She had no interest in the Professor or his pictures; she was unmoved by the persuasive Frenchman at her side—but together they offered a temporary escape. Suddenly, she resolved to avail herself of it.

She turned to look at Monsieur Reynaud.

'If I stayed, I don't think you'd get your pictures. But I'm willing to do what I can.'

'You are going to stay?' he asked eagerly.

'Yes.'

'You ... I should not remind you of these things, but as you are being kind, I shall be honest: shall you be able to bear this crazy

52

Professor? He is a rude fellow; he insults one. And this terrible cottage ... but there I can be of use; I can bring you some things to make you more comfortable.'

'No, thank you. I'll manage.'

'But food! I am told by Red that—'

'That won't worry me. I live on chicken and salad too.' She rose. 'You ought to give Red a bonus.'

'I shall indeed.'

'Are you going in to talk to the Professor?'

'No more. No. I am tired of trying to talk to the Professor. I shall say frankly, Lucille, that I do not envy you your hours in his company. You are an angel, and I am selfish to have condemned you to this—but one day, I promise that I will repay you. I know that it means leaving your agency and—'

'I was leaving the agency anyway; I was going on holiday.'

He looked, for the first time, somewhat at a loss.

'Of course, I did not know this. It is a wretched complication.'

'No, it isn't. I was going to an aunt in Paris. I can put her off.'

And she would be furious, but perhaps it was time to break the habit of agreeing to everything her aunt asked.

'If you are in Paris, we shall meet there and I will try to make your visit agreeable,' he said. 'It will be a great pleasure to be in Paris

53

with you.'

He must, she thought, have said the words a hundred times to a hundred women, but he could still make them sound warm and intimate. The pleasure, she decided, wouldn't be all on his side; going round Paris with him would be quite an experience.

She stopped as they were walking towards his car.

'Are you going to London?' she asked.

'Yes. I can take you?'

'I've got to get some luggage.'

'I will take you there and I will bring you back again.'

'No. If you'll drop me somewhere near my flat, I'll be grateful.'

They drove to town in his car, stopping on the way to lunch at a roadhouse. She enjoyed the drive, enjoyed the company, enjoyed the meal; she also enjoyed the conversation which, on Paul Reynaud's part, was a gently persistent attempt to extract some facts about her history and background, and on her part, the deliberate vagueness she had perfected over the years and used primarily to keep a discreet distance between herself and her staff.

He left her at the entrance to the block of flats in which she lived.

'To say "thank you" will be an understatement,' he said earnestly. 'You are doing more for me than you realise. If the Professor annoys you, assaults you, send for me.' He smiled. 'But I think that if blood is spilt, it will be the Professor's and not yours.'

She watched him drive away, and went up in the lift and let herself into her flat. It looked as she had left it: neat, impersonal, unlived-in. It had looked like this for six years; there was no reason to stand and stare at it—but she continued to stand and stare. She was seeing it in a way she had not seen it before.

Efficiency ... You could be efficient, she decided, without knowing how to climb hills or light archaic stoves or ride mares. All the same, she might as well admit that she hadn't shown up too well yesterday. Perhaps, in moving away from the muddle of her early years, she had moved too far. Perhaps, if her father had lived longer, she would have come to a better understanding of his merits, his value, his position in the world of music.

She felt a sudden need for reassurance. She went to the telephone and dialled the office number; reassurance came with the crisp, alert voice of her principal assistant.

'The Lucille Abbey Secretarial Agency. Can I help you?'

'This is Mrs Abbey. I didn't get off to Paris yesterday. For the moment, will you forward my personal letters to my flat, please? I'll leave the forwarding address with the porter.'

'Very well, Mrs Abbey. Anything else?'

'No, thanks. If anything unusual comes up, leave it until I get back, will you?'

'Very well.'

'Things going all right?'

'Yes, everything's fine. Nothing to report—oh, except that that Professor telephoned about half an hour ago.'

'Professor?'

'Professor Hallam. The one who—'

'Yes, I remember. What did he want?'

'He said he was ringing up to tell us he didn't want any more secretaries. He said the four we sent were no use. I pointed out that we'd only sent three, but he insisted that there was a fourth who had—he said—come and gone as fast as the others. I think we can write him off as slightly crazy.'

'More than slightly. Was that all he said?'

'He made some disparaging remarks about poor Mrs Adamson and Miss Clarkson and Olivia Bell. I didn't pass them on.'

'Good. Well, goodbye. I'll write and let you know when I'm returning.'

'Goodbye, Mrs Abbey. Happy holiday.'

Lucille put down the receiver reluctantly; she had the feeling that she was cutting herself off from all that was reasonable, normal, efficient. She would find none of these at Hill House.

She next spoke to Malcolm Donne. He was not pleased to hear that she was still in England; he liked, he said, to keep track of her; he had tracked her to Paris and was annoyed at having to back-track. His voice was firmer,

56

more decided, more abrupt than usual; she had told him that it was an addressing-the-meeting voice. Ladies and gentlemen, I need not tell you how worthy a cause has brought us here tonight...

'How long is this thing going to hold you up?' he asked.

'Two or three weeks; I can't tell you for certain.'

'But how about your aunt? Won't she find this a bit high handed? After all, I daresay she'd made her plans, too. If it comes to that, so had I; I'd booked a flight for Tuesday, to go over and see you.'

'I'm sorry. You can get the date changed, can't you?'

'I could if I knew what date to change it to. Are you sure you haven't allowed yourself to be caught up unnecessarily?'

'Quite sure. I sent three secretaries down to this job, and they wouldn't stay—so I'm going myself.'

'Where did you say it was?'

'A place called Holme.'

'Never heard of it. What makes you think you can do what three secretaries couldn't?'

'If you're going to be angry, I'll ring off.'

'I'm just trying to get myself straight, that's all; you've blown my plans to hell. I was coming over to Paris to give you some rather interesting news.'

'Well, tell me now.'

57

'It's not definite yet—that is, I haven't signed anything and neither have they. But I think we can say that the farm's ours.'

A chill crept over her.

'You bought it?'

'As good as.'

'But I thought we were going to look at it again before—'

'—before deciding? I didn't want to lose the chance of getting a good property at a good price, which is what would have happened if we'd spent too much time arguing. You liked it; I liked it; it's ours.'

'You're going to commute?'

'No. I'm going to give up the office and do what I've always wanted to do—settle down in the country.'

She closed her eyes. The farm was called Pheasants. There were splendid buildings for the animals and an indifferent house for the owners. Settle down in the country...

'Are you still there?' he asked.

'Yes. Wasn't the house rather ugly?'

'We'll get a firm of architects on to it. I was going to talk to you about it, lay it all out, ask your advice—and now you're running out on me and on your aunt. You're actually going to move down to this place?'

'Yes.'

'Comfortable quarters, I hope.'

'A cottage to myself.'

'Good. I'll run down and see you.'

58

'I wouldn't do that. The house is at the top of a hill, and the road up to it would tear your car tyres to bits. The less I'm distracted, the sooner I'll get the job done. I'll phone you when I'm free.'

'Well, don't sound so businesslike; haven't you a kind word to throw at me?'

She could almost see him smiling. She could almost see his face—handsome in a heavy way, with keen grey eyes, thick hair, thick black eyebrows. Strangers took him for a soldier; he was tall, he carried himself well and had a commanding air.

'I'll keep the kind words until I see you,' she said.

'I'm going to miss you. Don't get into mischief.'

She promised that she would not, and rang off; there was no need to caution him, for he was not a man who would get into mischief.

She put the future, the farm, resolutely from her mind. She had a bath and put on a sweater and slacks and re-packed her suitcase with country clothes—something she had not needed until she had met Malcolm.

Before leaving the flat, she picked up the telephone once more and sent a telegram to her aunt in Paris. One lie, she reflected, would save many explanations; she said merely that she was detained and would wire when she was free. Then, suitcase in one hand and her portable typewriter in the other, she let herself

59

out of the flat and made her way down to the street.

The mare was waiting at the farm. Lucille stared at it thoughtfully for some time; it seemed a pity to ignore the challenge in the animal's gaze. Then, with decisive movements, she took her typewriter to the farm and left it there. Leading the mare to a fallen tree trunk, she managed to hoist up her suitcase, and herself after it.

'Giddup,' she ordered.

The mare looked in the direction of the village and seemed to hesitate.

'He's walking,' Lucille explained. 'Now get going, and take it easy.'

Perhaps the weight of the suitcase kept the mare to a sober pace; perhaps those hours on Hector's back hadn't, after all, been a waste of money. Or perhaps—fantastic thought!—she was cut out, after all, to be a countrywoman.

CHAPTER THREE

It was always best, Lucille thought, to begin as one meant to go on. She meant to go on being comfortable; the Professor's absence in town gave her a good opportunity to begin.

She unpacked her suitcase in the cottage. Putting on an apron, she went over to the kitchen of the house and returned with mop and broom. She cleared the cottage of all furniture except the bed, carrying the things to a disused outbuilding; then she scrubbed, swept, dusted, washed the lavatory and brought the bathtub to a state in which she felt she could bear to use it. Then she made a tour of all the rooms in the house which were not locked. Every one was crammed with furniture and ornaments: vases, china figures, statuettes in wood, in ivory, jade and ebony. The task of listing, she realised, was going to prove a great deal more formidable than she had supposed— but she would worry about that later. For the moment, her aim was to make the cottage comfortable. Going through the rooms again, she chose a low easy chair, a small round table, a larger one to serve as desk, an embroidered footstool and three rugs. Arranging these to her satisfaction in the cottage, she went back to the house for some delicate, pale green cups and saucers, breakfast plates in pale shades of pottery and a variety of jars and containers which she arranged on the cottage shelves. She selected copper saucepans, a small copper kettle and some sharp knives; these, with other aids to cooking, she placed neatly above the stove.

She was beginning to feel at home; only the bed, bold and brassy, irritated her. She fetched a carved screen from the drawing-room; it was heavy, and awkward to manoeuvre round corners, but she got it into the cottage and, somewhat breathless, screened the bed and then walked to the door to observe the whole effect.

It was a startling transformation—but without the fire's glow, the cottage failed to come to life. She had used all the available wood, but there was a faint spark still glowing; coaxing it, blowing and holding newspapers against the bars, she saw at last a small flame; the rest was merely a matter of carrying over the Professor's supply of firewood from the study.

She was warm. She was surrounded by good furniture. She would eat off charming plates. It was a pity there was a window-pane missing; she would speak to Red about having it replaced.

It was dusk before the Professor returned. She left her chair reluctantly; she had just settled down after a satisfying meal of chicken omelette followed by cheese followed by fruit and cream followed by coffee. She wondered, as she walked outside to meet him, whether he would remember who she was; his memory seemed to her to have its off-moments.

He looked warm; he was carrying his jacket over his arm. As she came out of the cottage, he halted and stared at her blankly.

'Good evening, Professor.'

There was a pause; she waited for him to place her.

'Was it you who took the mare?' he

demanded at last.

'Yes. Didn't they tell you? I left my typewriter at the farm.'

'I didn't go to the farm. Why didn't you come up in the cart? Come to think of it, why did you come up here at all?'

'I decided to take the job.'

'I didn't offer you the job. I told you quite distinctly—and I made a point of telling that agency, too—that I did not—'

'Have you had dinner?'

'Look, my dear young lady, don't try those high-handed tricks with me,' he said angrily. 'I forget trifling matters now and then, but I remember quite well the interview I had with you. Something made you change your mind. Did that French fellow bribe you?'

'Monsieur Reynaud? No, he didn't. I decided to stay. If I don't suit you, you can sack me—but it's only reasonable to give me a trial. Have you eaten anything? If not, I can—'

'I don't have dinner. I have bread and cheese and beer. I hope you understand that if you're going to stay, you'll be responsible for getting all your own meals?'

'Of course. I presume Red will bring up anything I order?'

'Yes. Will you kindly tell me why you took the mare?'

'You told me I was out of practice. What time do you like to start work in the mornings?'

'I start at eight, but I don't want to be

disturbed; I'll let you know when I need you. And as you've obviously been approached by that French fellow, let's get one thing clear: I don't want him hanging round pestering me about pictures. And one thing more: I don't want to hear complaints from you about the cottage.'

'I'm sure I shall manage to make myself comfortable,' she assured him. 'Goodnight, Professor.'

With a curt nod, he went into the house and closed the door—without, she noted resentfully, so much as an enquiry as to whether she had had anything to eat or drink; without one thought for her comfort or well-being, without any offer of wood or hot water. It was as well that she knew how to take care of herself.

She had taken care of herself extremely well. She had helped herself to cold chicken, the last of the lettuce, the remains of an excellent Camembert, a small bottle of wine, tea, coffee and bread and butter. Arrayed on the shelves of her little cottage cupboard were honey and marmalade, salt, pepper, fruit, tomatoes; she had a good supply of potatoes. She had tableclothes and napkins; she had the Professor's wood; the kettle was warming for her hot water bottle. She got ready for bed, piled on enough wood to last through the night and then climbed between the sheets.

After an interval, she heard the Professor's

footsteps marching across to the cottage; she heard, and ignored, his angry thundering on the door. He was no doubt looking for the chicken and the coffee and the Camembert.

He went away. She hoped he would go hungry to bed.

She had set the alarm for seven o'clock. She woke to the sound of wind and rain, but the cottage was snug enough; all she needed, she thought, was a canary singing in a cage and a cat to curl up in front of the stove. She heard the arrival of Red and Roz, and opened the window to see them swathed in oilskins and sou-westers. They handed in her typewriter and she gave Red a slip of paper.

'My order,' she said.

Red glanced at it and whistled in surprise.

'What—all that lot?' he exclaimed. 'The Professor'll take off; he likes to keep the bills down.'

'Secretaries have to eat,' Lucille pointed out. 'Give him the bill for the food, and let me have the bill for the sherry and the nuts and the olives.'

'Not the wine?'

'Not the wine. Secretaries have to drink. And don't bawl up at the Professor's window tomorrow; I'll have his list ready for you.'

'Can I bawl today?'

'Certainly.'

She closed the window, only to find him peering through the aperture.

'I took a bet with Roz,' he told her. 'An' I won it.'

'Congratulations.'

'Know what it was? I bet her Mr Reynaud would make you stay. He's got a way, hasn't he?'

'He wound me round his little finger. Will you please go away? And don't forget to have that pane put in.'

She made herself some coffee and then dressed and got out the two reference books she had brought from her flat—books that had belonged to her mother. They gave elementary but helpful information on furniture and the types of wood used in furniture-making; periods and makes were clearly set out. Some facts she knew; others were new to her. She grew so absorbed in her reading that she did not hear the Professor's knock on her door.

He came in holding a sheaf of papers.

'Type these, will you?'

'Good morning, Professor.'

'Ah. Original and one copy, and let me have them as soon as possible,' he directed.

He went out without giving a glance round him, and she resolved that soon she would teach him to say goodnight and good morning, and perhaps even please and thank you.

She worked until half past twelve; then she unpacked and put away the stores that Red had placed inside the door. She sat down at one o'clock to ham, tongue, hard-boiled eggs, bread and cheese and salad. She was eating with keen enjoyment when the Professor came in search of her.

'Those notes—' he began, and stopped, astounded. '*Eating!*'

'One o'clock is my lunch hour,' she informed him.

'But ... but the work I gave you—'

She nodded towards the typing table.

'The finished work is in that file. You can have the rest this afternoon. I always take an hour and and a half for lunch.'

He made no reply. His eyes were glazed, taking in the changes she had made.

'Nice, don't you think?' she asked him. 'You ought to be grateful; I've saved you from being had up for misrepresentation.'

He was looking at the meal.

'Ham ... tongue ... You were right,' he said. 'You know how to look after yourself.'

' "The labourer is worthy", and so on. Have you cooked your potatoes yet?'

'I eat when my work is finished.'

'Well, this is all your food—that is, you pay for it. If you care to join me, do.'

Without a word, he drew up a chair and took his place at the table. He was stretching out a hand to help himself when she stopped him.

'One moment.'

Rising, she brought plates, a glass and a napkin.

'If you're lunching with me,' she told him,

67

'you'll have to observe a few formalities. Where have you lived—at the zoo?'

'I've lived alone.'

'So have I. People who live alone have to guard against becoming savages. Will you put your table napkin on your knee, please—or would you like me to tie it round your neck?'

'Women like you,' he said coldly, 'very often end up with something tied—extremely tightly—round their necks. Is that the cheese you took last night? If so, I'd be glad if you'd return what's left of it. It was a rather special cheese.'

'It certainly was,' she agreed. 'But you told me to look after myself, and that's what I'm doing. I shall expect you to provide the same food and wine that I have when I'm at home.'

'Can you seriously expect a busy professor to run after you?'

'No. I know all about busy professors. The more you know of them, the less you expect from them.'

He looked up from his food and gave her a look in which she detected for the first time a faint stirring of interest.

'I haven't got round to finding out who you are,' he said. 'Perhaps we can begin at the beginning. You're Mrs...'

'Abbey. I run the agency you applied to—the one you phoned yesterday. They all think you're crazy, and with good reason.'

'Where is your husband?'

'I haven't the faintest idea.'

'You left him?'

'I divorced him. Abbey's my maiden name.'

'You didn't remarry?'

'I'm going to.'

Had she said that? She wondered in amazement. Had she really spoken the words, and with such certainty sounding in them, such finality? The reason for this apparent sweeping away of all her doubts must, she thought, be the Professor himself; in contrast to his unalluring appearance and total lack of graces, any man would seem a prize.

'Where's your fiancé?'

'I'm meeting him in Paris as soon as I've done this job.'

'How old are you?'

'Twenty-eight.'

'How often do you take over from your defecting secretaries?'

'This is the first time.'

'All because you swallowed that Frenchman's story of wanting to buy my mother's pictures? Good as you are at taking care of yourself, let me warn you that there's something fishy about that fellow. My mother's pictures aren't worth the canvas they're painted on.'

'It's your opinion against a well-known art expert's. If you don't want the pictures, why not let him take them away at whatever price you agree on? Why keep him hanging about?

69

He's prepared to accept your terms; he's—'

'In the first place,' said the Professor, holding out his plate for replenishment, 'nobody asked him to come here. No pictures, or anything else, were as yet for sale. On the day that I discovered my father's papers, this self-styled art expert came here in his showy car, tracked me to my study, told me a cock-and-bull story of my mother having offered to sell him some pictures, and expected me to put aside everything and attend to him. He may have impressed you—he's a handsome chap—but he didn't impress me. His story was full of holes. My mother enjoyed painting, but she had, I'm thankful to say, no great opinion of her own work. Anybody who was unwise enough, insincere enough, rash enough to admire one of her pictures hanging on her walls, was liable to find himself holding it—she'd merely take it down and make a present of it. She wasn't in need of money; my father kept her liberally supplied. Why would she walk in and offer her pictures to this or that gallery? And if she did, why should I interrupt valuable work in order to accommodate any potential buyer who appears at my door?—Why did you say you knew all about professors? Was your husband one?'

'No. My father.'

'Abbey ... Abbey.' The Professor searched his memory. 'Clement Abbey?'

'Yes.'

'Medieval Church music?'

'Yes.'

'Not my line, but I knew his name. Didn't he bring out an important work before he died?'

'He took eight years to write a book of about two hundred pages; that works out at about twenty-five pages a year.'

'It works out at exactly twenty-five pages a year. Are you trying to say he was wasting his time?'

'How many people have read, or will read his book? During those eight years, he had a daughter to look after—me. So he went up to his study every morning and stayed there until late at night, and in due course produced his work on plainsong chants and motets and polyphonic music.'

'So that was how you learned to look after yourself? You're indicating that he ought to have given up his pursuit of knowledge and attended to his domestic duties. Well, it's been said before, but there are men—my father was one—who are driven to dig deeper than others in their search for truth. You won't approve of those notes you've been typing this morning— your criterion seems to be based on sales figures. But the science of government fascinated my father. He considered that political theory was the base of all search for man's prosperity—moral and material. His posthumous book won't be read by many, but it'll be read by serious thinkers, and it will

71

advance their knowledge. So I'd be grateful if you'd give your mind to it, and let Monsieur whatever-he-styles-himself wait until we have more time to spare for him.'

'Why didn't you keep on the housekeeper?'

'Because I didn't need her. What are you getting up for? You haven't had your full hour and a half.'

'You've got wood to chop—didn't you promise to keep me supplied?'

He went to the door, and she called him back.

'You forgot to say thank you,' she reminded him.

'For lunch?'

'Yes.'

'Didn't you point out that it was all my own food? Do I have to thank you for letting me eat it?'

'Would it hurt you to say please and thank you, once in a while?'

'Hurt? I daresay not. Please let me thank you for my food.'

The door banged. She went back to work consoling herself with the reflection that she would take care to disabuse him of the notion that all his meals would be taken with her. From that day, she set the pattern of her days, and he had to accept it. He could find no fault with her work; she was quick, accurate and thorough. She stopped each day at a quarter to five; the rest of the time was her own.

For exercise, she walked down the hill, sometimes to Holme village but mostly to the farm. From the children's widowed grandmother she learned the history not only of the farm family, but also the Professor's.

It was his grandfather who had bought the hill and, against all advice, built the house at the top. It would, expert opinion said, fall down as soon as it was put up; it was being built too close to the edge, and without sufficient support. The house had not come down; only the little Greek-style temple and its gardens had come down, on a night that had made local history. The story was told and retold; scarcely a word varied. Lucille came to name it The Time the Temple Toppled. She caught something of the terror and excitement, felt the bitter cold, heard the screams of servants as they fled from the house, fearing it would follow the temple down the hill-side. Today, the farm children were reaping the harvest of the avalanche of masonry; they dug up fragments of the shattered statues and carried them to an uncle who, they explained to Lucille, had a junk shop in Southampton and liked to exhibit, among his other wares, pieces of the soil-encrusted marble.

'Takes people in,' pointed out Red.

'You mean your uncle *sells* the bits?'

'Well, not exactly. What he does,' Red said, 'is to leave them sort of lying about. People pick them up, and uncle says they're not worth

73

anything. That only eggs 'em on; he tells them to name a price, and they do, and he shares with us, fifty-fifty.'

'Do you call that honest?' demanded Lucille.

'It's business, my uncle says. And money's money, isn't it?'

Money was certainly money to everybody on the farm. They were ready with glasses of milk—but they charged for them. They offered to knit, to sew, to bake—at a price. They served the Professor, but he paid adequately for the service.

Money was also money to Monsieur Reynaud; every other day he came to seek out Lucille, to remind her of the need for haste. He came after working hours, driving the car himself, bringing flowers so expensive, so exotic that they looked out of place in the cottage. He seldom went up the hill; he waylaid Lucille down at the farm and enquired how the Professor's work was progressing. His persistence amazed her—and disturbed her; he was waiting day by day for the chance of carrying away pictures which the Professor declared to be daubs. She found herself almost as anxious to open Mrs Hallam's rooms as Monsieur Reynaud himself.

She was able, at the end of ten days, to assure him that in a day or two more the work of transcribing the Professor's notes would be done.

'And then—the pictures?' he asked.

'Yes.'

'I shall come tomorrow.'

'Not tomorrow. The day after.'

There was a visitor the next day, but it was not Monsieur Reynaud. Red, giving Lucille a lift up the hill towards evening, hazarded a description.

'She was thin, and good-looking, and smart—but she looked cheesed off about something. You should've seen her car! Jag. She thought twice about taking it up the hill, but it was either that or the cart, and Roz said her suit must've cost more than the tyres, that's why she just took one look at the cart seats and decided to drive up.'

'When was this?'

'An hour ago, more or less. I thought she was a friend of the Professor, but she asked me who lived at the house. Professor Hallam, I said. You could tell she'd never heard of him, but she went up; I offered to go up and take her to the Professor, but she didn't want me. I wish I could've got into the car.'

She got out at the top and thanked him for the lift. He seemed to feel that if he hung about, he might glean some news to carry down to the farm; under Lucille's bland gaze, however, he turned the cart and went reluctantly down the hill.

She walked to the cottage and opened the door. Before she could enter, she heard the Professor's footsteps and turned to hear his

75

angry question.

'Did you meet that madwoman?'

'No. Red told me someone came in a Jaguar.'

'I don't know what she came in. She caught me just as I was coming out of the house—like a fool, I let her in.'

He followed Lucille into the cottage, poked the fire and slumped on to a chair.

'What did she want?' Lucille asked.

'She was looking for her fiancé.'

'Here?'

'Here. Not her fiancé; no. She'd broken it off. Her ex-fiancé.'

'And could you produce him for her?'

'It's not at all funny. She was in a state, and she had a piercing voice. Having told her that I knew nothing of her fiancé, I expected that she would go away—but she didn't. She waved a paper at me, and she cried. Why do women always end by crying?'

'Why did she come here looking for him?'

'Because, having burgled her house, or her mother's house, he left a clue—the torn-off top of a letter with the address of this house—Hill House—printed on it. The paper was the paper my mother always used. This woman found it and jumped to the conclusion that he was here, or was known by somebody here.'

'He burgled her house?'

'It appears that, having been engaged to her for some months, he knew something about

76

her habits. He knew that she and her mother spent every August away from the house. He had a latchkey. He let himself in and helped himself to a valuable collection of china. She came back before her mother, found that the china had gone, found the address of this house, and came here expecting to find out something about him.'

'Why didn't she go to the police?'

'For reasons connected with the manner in which her mother acquired the china. A charming lot, don't you think?'

Lucille frowned in thought.

'But why *did* he have the address of this house?' she asked.

'How do I know? That's what this woman kept asking me.'

'What was her name?'

The Professor groped in his mind—unsuccessfully.

'I don't remember. She wrote it down—it'll be somewhere in my study.'

'What's *his* name?'

'I've no idea. I wasn't listening with every nerve strained. All I wanted was to get her out of the house. I said that if they didn't care to call in the police, she might consider using a firm of private detectives to trace this chinaman.'

'But there must be some connection—mustn't there?'

'I don't follow you.'

77

'Why would he have this address? And if he had this address, and if he's a person who goes round helping himself to other people's property when they're away from home, how do you know he hasn't been here? The house was closed for a time, wasn't it?'

'Not for long. And what is there in it to attract thieves?'

'A lot of good furniture, and a number of good ornaments. And—'

She stopped, and he prompted her.

'And what?'

'According to Monsieur Reynaud, you've also got some good pictures.'

'My mother's?' For the first time, she heard him laugh—a deep, throaty, infectious sound. 'Steal my mother's pictures?' He sobered. 'Obviously, it's time you saw them for yourself. You can tell your friend the Frenchman that any time after tomorrow, he can come and take his pick. The only person who ever thought those pictures worth a second glance was the housekeeper—Mrs Westover—who described them, with perfect sincerity, as sweetly pretty. They were, in fact, far from pretty; my mother's preference was for painting mountains, and most of her pictures look like decorative temperature charts. If she'd been a less honest woman, she would have left the pictures to Mrs Westover in her will; knowing them to be worthless, she left her, instead, a tidy sum of money. She gave her, of course, the odd picture for a birthday, or for Christmas.'

Lucille tried to picture the Professor's mother surrounded by the artists she liked to befriend, painting mountains, packing up the canvases and bringing them home to be framed and hung on the walls. She had died on her way home from France; perhaps she had seen Monsieur Reynaud; perhaps she had not.

The Professor's voice recalled her.

'Are you dreaming? I've spoken to you twice.'

'What about?'

'Bills. Food bills. Bills for all these stores you've been ordering. You've been here less than two weeks and you've spent more than I spend in six months.'

'You told me I could make my own arrangements with Red.'

'I meant that you were at liberty to order a reasonable amount of food—as I do. I was looking through the bills when that woman interrupted me. Grapes, frozen prawns, fillet of steak—fillet of steak! Do you know what that costs?'

'Yes. Would you like to stay and have some now?'

'Fillet of steak?'

'Preceded by prawns fried in batter. I'll give you a drink and you can sit and watch me getting it ready.'

'I feel sorry,' he said, leaning back in his chair, drink in hand, 'for that fellow you're

79

marrying. I hope he's rich.'

'He's going to farm. We shall probably have fillets on the hoof—and he'll notice what he's eating; he likes good food. I wish you'd break your boiled potato habits.'

'You wish I'd break some of my other habits, too. Such as walking off without making a speech. Do I have to have an exit line, like an actor?'

'Why can't you be polite, like other people?'

'Other people are polite? I can't say I've noticed it. You weren't polite when you came to see me first. That Frenchman as good as called me crazy. And why should one do as other people do? The sole reason my grandfather built this house, the sole reason my father lived in it, was to get away from people. They needed, and I need, freedom to work. They could do without, and I can do without, the meaningless thronging that's called being sociable. The only people I want round me are colleagues; people with ideas to exchange, on one's own or on any other subject. Life, as I like to live it, is too short to waste at parties. Some poor devils have to give them and other poor devils have to go to them: entertainers, for example, who can't risk getting out of the public eye; fellows who have things to sell and tout them in drawing-rooms; old ladies of both sexes who want to gossip. They're all only too happy to drink second-rate drink and eat messy titbits and wear out their friends' carpets. But not me. I want everybody to be thoroughly happy doing whatever they want to do, even if it's only wasting life's golden hours—but I want them to do it without me. Have I made myself clear?'

'You've practically exhausted the subject.'

'By no means. I'm merely trying to convey my point of view.'

'You've conveyed it. Did you look through those lists I left on your desk?'

'I did. You appear to know something about furniture.'

'I'm glad. I'm looking it up as I go along. Perhaps, after dinner, you'd let me have some of the keys. It's time you let Monsieur Reynaud off the hook. Would you put the cloth on the table, please?'

Clumsily, he obeyed her.

'And the napkins and glasses and that little bowl of flowers,' she directed.

'Do we really have to go to these lengths to sit down to prawns and steak?'

'Yes, we really do.'

'Shall I lower the lights?'

'No. You only have to do that when you've noticed the woman you're with. Let's keep the lights on, and I'll sit where you can see me.'

'I seem to remember telling you, when you first came, that you wouldn't distract me. I am fortunately able to—'

'—remain undistracted. Knives and forks, please. Do you like butter with your bread?'

81

'Yes; always.'

'Don't say yes always; say yes please.'

'Yes, please. Has your whole life been passed in training people to perform minuets?'

'You're the first person I've ever met who can be truthfully described as un-housetrained. White wine with your prawns?'

'How could you cool white wine sufficiently in this warm room?'

'It's outside the window; will you fetch it, please?'

He brought it and poured it out. Walking round the table, he drew out her chair and held it for her.

'How's this?' he asked.

She sat down.

'It's a beginning,' she said.

'It's a pity you won't be able to stay until I complete the syllabus. I shall miss you,' he said musingly. 'You're beautiful. You have a skin, a figure, a voice that could stir a man. When I was an undergraduate, I used to watch the men round me competing to win the favours of women like you—to the great detriment of their studies. I made up my mind that until I met a woman whom I knew, without any doubt, that I could mate with and work with, I would keep myself—'

'Undistracted.'

'Quite so. It was comparatively easy in your case, because you have such a bad temper. You would never, I'm certain, leave a man free to

82

get on with his work in his own way; you would keep taking him out and polishing him. Am I required to tell you that these prawns are very well done?'

'You're improving; a week ago, you wouldn't have noticed. When the typing's done, do you want me to stay and help you list the contents of the house?'

'Not if you're anxious to join your fiancé in Paris. Without you, I would have taken a good deal longer over my father's work; as it is, I've time enough to go through the house and do everything that has to be done.'

'In that case, I'll go as soon as I've done the last of the notes.'

He said nothing. With sinking heart, she realised that she did not want to go. Up here, she had felt a thousand miles away from Paris, from Malcolm, from the farm that he was busy buying. She had felt secure, out of reach, safe. She had got used to the Professor; she no longer thought his appearance odd. She felt well and braced in the strong air. She liked the farm and the children, the rides in the cart, her hours in the cottage. She had to go; life, real life, lay down there at the bottom of the hill. She had to go—to Paris, to Malcolm, to marriage, to the future and whatever it might bring.

But she did not want to go.

She went, at the conclusion of the meal, to get the keys from the Professor. In his study, he opened one drawer and then another and then another; from each he drew out keys, some large, some small, some new, some old and rusty. There were keys on rings, keys tied together with string or tape, single keys, keys fitted into padlocks. Not one key was labelled.

'You can see,' the Professor said, 'what the Frenchman was asking. It wasn't a case simply of opening a door. If you can find the keys to my mother's rooms, you'll be clever; I doubt if I could pick them out of that assortment.'

Lucille stared at him in amazement.

'But ... but why on earth did the housekeeper leave all the keys like this, without a single label?'

'I think I told you she was a silly woman. It probably didn't occur to her that she would be the only person who'd know which key fitted which door or drawer or cupboard or cabinet or chest.'

'It looks to me like spite—to pay you out for not keeping her on.'

'No. She wasn't spiteful. Muddled, but not malicious. Well, there they are.'

It took her—she timed it—four hours to disentangle the keys. The sorting took a day. During the latter part of it, Monsieur Reynaud was at her elbow. He picked out, a hundred times, a key which he thought would fit the key of Mrs Hallam's rooms; each time, he was wrong. His self-control, up to now so admirable, so extraordinary, seemed to Lucille

84

to be slipping. He became impatient; he muttered and then railed at the incompetence which was responsible for holding him up in the last stage of his quest.

They found—Lucille, the Professor and Monsieur Reynaud together—no key which would open the rooms they were trying to get into. They searched the house for more keys, and found none. They were forced, at last, to admit that the keys to the rooms containing the pictures were missing. Red was sent down to the village in Monsieur Reynaud's car, and returned with a locksmith, who went to work at once.

The door, creaking slightly, opened at last. They went past the workman and stood, three of them, in a sitting-room; beyond, when the Professor had thrown open the shutters, they saw the bedroom.

There was a good deal of furniture; there were too many ornaments. Round the walls of both the sitting-room and bedroom they saw squares of various sizes—squares of a colour brighter than the rest of the walls, proving that frames had hung there.

But of pictures—in the sitting-room and the bedroom, in every other room they examined—there was not a single one.

CHAPTER FOUR

Paris was still full of tourists. Lucille could see them, camera-slung, casually attired, from the windows of the taxi that was taking her to her aunt's shop. Some of them, she presumed, were hastening on to the next place on their itinerary; some of them, she hoped, would stay to experience the trembling excitement that had coursed through her when she first saw the buildings whose outlines were familiar to all the world: the Madeleine, the Louvre, the Tuileries. She remembered still her first drive up the Avenue de l'Opera; she could recall with equal clarity her sensations as she walked for the first time along the Avenue des Champs-Elysées.

She had explored all Paris as some of the tourists appeared to be doing now; she had grown familiar with the Passy district, on the fringe of which was her aunt's shop, situated in a narrow, tree-shaded street, one end of which joined a busy, fashionable avenue. Called the Rue des Dames, it seemed to have been forgotten in the frenzy of planning that had raised all round it monsters of steel and cement; the little shops on both sides of the road still looked out upon lovely trees, ancient cobbles and crookedly-hanging, real lamps.

Lucille had come to know and like all the

shop-owners; they lived, as did her aunt, in the little flats above their shops. All except her aunt were old-established tenants, some of them claiming descent from the families who had opened the first shops in the reign of the Sun King. She knew Monsieur Perron, who owned the well-stocked little charcuterie; the Didrons farther down at the épicerie; the brothers Le Moine—barbers—and their friend Monsieur Lachaise, who owned the book shop at the corner, next door to her aunt, and who was half-envied, half-pitied because his shop front faced not the quiet little Rue des Dames, but the brash, busy avenue. On the other side of her aunt's shop was the hat shop owned by Madame Baltard—such hats! Hats that could, that would, only be worn by true Parisiennes: frothy, fantastic, challengingly feminine.

But it was not of Madame Baltard's hats that she was thinking as she stared out of the taxi windows at the rain-washed Paris streets. Her mind was back at Hill House and on the mystifying, unsatisfactory end to her work for the Professor. She was remembering the long-awaited entry into Mrs Hallam's rooms, the blank spaces on the walls and the Professor's momentary consternation; most vividly of all she was remembering Monsieur Reynaud's face, suddenly ugly in its naked rage, dark and contorted. Glancing at him, she had hastily averted her eyes—and she had understood how certain he had been that he would get the pictures in the end.

She and the Professor had opened all the rooms; they had searched the house from ground floor to attics. Monsieur Reynaud, recovering some of his poise, had assisted them, combing every room for a sign of the pictures for which he had waited. Watching him, she had come to disbelieve and disregard the Professor's reiterated statements regarding their lack of value; Monsieur Reynaud's manner convinced her that they were very valuable indeed.

He had realised at last that the pictures were not in the house. Then the housekeeper, he asserted, had stolen them. She had carried them away—they were not large—in one of the trunks which Red had placed in the cart and driven to the station.

The Professor had agreed that Mrs Westover might have taken the pictures—but that did not mean, he said, that they had been stolen. There had been no mention of pictures in his mother's will, but it was more than likely that, knowing the housekeeper's unaccountable admiration for her work, she had made her a present of them. It would have been quite in keeping with her character and impulsive habits.

Monsieur Reynaud had made no comment; he had merely asked for the address to which Mrs Westover had gone. It was Red who gave him the address in Canterbury to which Mrs

Westover had instructed him to send letters that might come for her after her departure. She was going, Red said, to live with a niece.

Throughout the confusion, Lucille had said nothing of the woman who had come to Hill House in search of a thief; she had nothing but theories to advance. But on Monsieur Reynaud's departure, she took from the Professor's study the paper on which the visitor had written her name and address, and then told the Professor that in her opinion it was there, and not at Canterbury, that Monsieur Reynaud should be conducting his search. She had not convinced the Professor; she had not even succeeded in interesting him in the subject. The only person who cared in the least where the pictures had got to was Monsieur Reynaud, who had made a great nuisance of himself and who now had mercifully departed, leaving him free to finish his work in the house and hand it over to the auctioneers.

'Let Mrs Westover keep the pictures,' he said. 'They'll give her the only pleasure they're ever likely to give anybody.'

'You're going to let her get away with something that might have brought you in a good deal of money?'

'That Frenchman wouldn't have given ten shillings for the lot. Forget it. Mrs Westover couldn't steal anything; she hasn't got the necessary cunning or courage.'

'Yet the only key that was missing was the key that opened the door of your mother's room. Doesn't that strike you as odd?'

'You strike me as odd. Are you concerned with my loss, or that Frenchman's?'

'With yours—because I think it's weak to allow yourself to be cheated.'

'It's hysterical to imagine villainy where no villainy exists.'

She had been unable to change his attitude, and at last had given up the attempt. He had given her a cheque, thanked her with formal, exaggerated politeness, settled her with her luggage in the cart and, she thought, with a curious sinking of the heart, forgotten her the moment she had been driven out of sight.

She would take longer to forget him. She would miss his caustic comments and his sudden appearances at the door of the cottage, food bills in hand, his long nose pointing accusingly at her. She would continue to see him snatching off his glasses and putting them on again; she would recall his maddening refusal to consider any point of view but his own. It was curious to feel regret at leaving a man who had given frequent signs of having forgotten her very presence—but miss him she would.

The taxi stopped; she found that she was not at Hill House, but in France; in the capital of France and in the heart of the capital, for this little street, short and in places shabby, existed only for the French. There was nothing here for the tourist; they might come and stare in wonder, but they would never have the courage to buy one of Madame Baltard's hats. Only one at a time was displayed in the window; Lucille could see it as she got out to pay the driver—shaped like a cornucopia, spilling grapes and cherries; at the top, a sprinkle of silver stars to show that Madame knew her mythology.

Her aunt's shop looked as trim as ever. Above, the flowing letters spelled out her business pseudonym: Madame Camille. In the window, a ladder of small glass shelves held the shop's wares: English cosmetics.

Opposite, in the doorway of his shop, Monsieur Perron stood smiling and bowing. From her aunt there was no sign; her aunt did not stand bowing in doorways. Next door, she was surprised and a little worried to see that Monsieur Lachaise's book shop was closed and shuttered; she hoped that nothing was amiss. They could not be away on holiday; nobody in the Rue des Dames, except her aunt, ever took a holiday; even Madame Baltard's shop remained open all summer long, though her clients had all left for their country estates.

Her suitcases were placed on the cobbles. A dozen neighbours came hurrying to welcome her; then she entered her aunt's shop.

Nothing seemed to have changed. The small, faintly-scented interior, the pale grey carpet, the delicate gilt chairs, the semicircular glass counter with a shelf below on which were arrayed pale pink, pale blue, black or mother-of-pearl jars containing the various makes of cosmetics—all was as she remembered it.

Here, for the past ten years, she had taken her annual holiday. Here she had acted as stand-in while her aunt went to St Jean de Luz.

She had been invited shortly after her father's death. She knew little of her aunt—widow of her father's brother—except what was known by all the family: her husband had died, leaving no money, and she had been left to make her way alone.

Nearly twenty years younger than her husband, she had been forty when he died. Orphaned early, she had been brought up by nuns in France; the marriage of the middle-aged bachelor had surprised his relations only a little less than the sight of his slim, pretty, shy little wife. At his death, it was revealed that they had been living for some time on the edge of penury; sometimes, Camille had confided, in answer to questions, there had been barely enough. Barely enough to eat, to drink, to dress, to pay bills.

If there had been barely enough for the couple, there was more than enough for the widow. Living in a tiny flat in London, busying herself with embroidery which she sold to friends, she made a picture of such charm and courage that the closest fists opened and dug into pockets. Women gave her presents of clothes; men brought flowers and sat in the softly-lit little drawing-room opposite the soft pink cheeks and the brave blue eyes, and went home to speak of pluck, of by-jove-a-game-little-woman, and to suggest taking the poor little thing when they went to Greece, to Italy or to Switzerland. Her gratitude was expressed in gentle tears and softly-pressed hands. When she announced the news of having inherited from an uncle a little property at Passy, there was a general move to encourage and assist her in her plan to set up shop for herself.

Lucille had been invited for a visit; not until her arrival had her aunt broached, delicately, hesitantly, the project of her taking over the shop each year for two or three weeks while her aunt went away for a rest. Anxious to help, glad to be assured of a free holiday, she had agreed—and it was only two years later, when she went to work for a time in the London office of a firm of accountants that she learned the extent and value of the investments that Mrs Camille Abbey had been making over the years—years that went back to the beginning of her marriage.

Lucille had said nothing to anybody regarding her discovery. Her aunt, like Robin Hood, had robbed only the rich; she had made her nest of feathers plucked from those who would not miss them. She had never liked her aunt; now she detested her, but she did not see herself in the role of denouncer. Never, she thought, could the art of cadging have been practised with greater success; nobody had ever cried poverty with a sweeter voice.

The uncle and the little inheritance at Passy had been twin myths; her aunt's instructions to the accountants to find and buy a small property in the Passy district had been explicit and businesslike. And it was interesting, having come to know the truth, to discover that the French had been almost as kind to the little widow as the English had been. That is, at first; lately, Lucille had noticed that Madame Camille was still respected, but she was not loved; perhaps her success was too evident. To those who visited her from time to time from England, she said that if her health did not break down, she hoped to pay off the mortgage within a reasonable time.

She came forward at Lucille's entry and turned a cheek to receive her niece's kiss.

'Well, my dearest? You're here at last. Let me look at you.' She studied Lucille affectionately. 'You look a little tired, but as charming as usual. Will you go upstairs and unpack? As soon as I've closed the shop, I'll be with you.'

Lucille had long ago grown accustomed to this double-talk. Going upstairs, she knew, meant unpacking, going into the little kitchen and preparing a meal. She liked cooking, but she did not enjoy preparing the kind of food her aunt liked; she had to make sauces, blanch tiny onions, chop parsley and spend a good deal of time turning the cheapest cuts of meat into palatable dishes. She thought nostalgically of the Professor's straight-forward system; closing her eyes, she could see steaming potatoes with butter melting on them, and milk foaming in a large glass jug.

She brought herself sharply back to the present, cooked dinner for herself and her aunt, and laid the table in the little dining-room. She heard her aunt come upstairs and go into her room; she emerged some time later in a dress of soft blue that matched her eyes and made her look young and defenceless.

'Lucille, my dear, you shouldn't have done all this,' she protested gently. 'You must be so tired after your journey. Shall we dine by candlelight? You don't need soft light, but I think at my age it's so much kinder, so much more flattering.'

Lucille lit the candles. They dined: soup, sole with a sauce, cheese, white wine, coffee. The silver gleamed, the crystal shone; it was all very pleasant, or would have been if everywhere Lucille looked she had not seen the Professor tearing with strong teeth at a chicken leg.

'Where have the Lachaises gone?' she asked her aunt. 'The shop was shuttered. Do you know where they are?'

Her aunt sighed gently.

'Yes, I know. They went to Lyons, I'm afraid—for good.'

'You don't mean to tell me they went bankrupt?'

Her aunt laughed—a sound of bells that made other people's laughter sound like the neighing of horses.

'Oh, my dear Lucille, what an idea! No, they didn't go bankrupt. But they weren't doing as well as they liked. I think they missed their son when he married and went to America; I don't think Monsieur Lachaise had ever expected to carry on the business alone. It isn't as though he had a mere trickle of customers, as I have.'

Lucille had wondered, once, whether—after discovering the truth about her aunt's finances—she would find the gently-uttered lies, the soft half-truths difficult to swallow. To her relief—because the annual trip to Paris was at that time helping her to endure the break-up of her marriage—she found herself merely amused.

'Who's going to take over their shop?' she enquired.

'Well...' Madame Camille refilled Lucille's glass and her own.

'Well what?'

'As a matter of fact, it had struck me that if only I could have moved to those corner premises, with that window straight on to the Avenue, I might have been able to do a little more business. Don't think I'm not grateful for

96

my little success; I *am*, Lucille, I *am*. But I have been cramped here; you can see that. Two people in the shop make it seem crowded.'

And so, Lucille said—but not aloud—you're expanding. You've bought out the Lachaises. Go ahead and tell it in your own way.

'It means, of course, a further mortgage. It means more struggle, more work. I know all that—but I feel that I *must* take my courage in my hands. It's now, Lucille dearest, or *never*. I am forty-eight. I went to feel that in a few years, I can relax, rest, take life a little more easily.'

'Expanding doesn't only mean more work,' Lucille pointed out. 'It means paying for an assistant. That's why I don't expand. You've got a sweet little shop and a flat which you've made beautiful—why not stay as you are?'

As if I didn't know, she continued to herself. Profits, profits and more profits...

'I need more storage space, Lucille. The shop on the corner has a basement, which none of these along this street have. I've always needed storage space.'

'Does anybody know what you intend to do? I mean, any of the other ... that is, any of the tradespeople along Rue des Dames?'

'There are *rumours*, of course. Several people wanted the place, as you can imagine. If I hadn't known dear old Madame Lachaise— his mother, you know, who was the real owner—if I hadn't paid her a little visit when I

97

heard they were selling up, I don't think I would have had any hope at all of—'

'—putting in a bid.'

'Dearest, you make it sound very cut-and-dried. I'm not a Big Businessman, you must remember. People in my position have to feel their way.'

So she had felt her way along to old Madame Lachaise and cut the ground from beneath her competitors.

'The risks,' she heard her aunt saying pensively, 'are enormous. It's tragic that I haven't a husband; a man to consult.'

'Why don't you ask Malcolm's advice?'

'Malcolm? Is this the Malcolm Donne you've mentioned to me?'

'Yes.'

'Do you mean that he's coming to Paris?'

'Yes.'

'To see Paris, or to see you?'

'Me, I suppose. I'll get him a room at the hotel along the Avenue. I promise not to let him disturb me during working hours. He'll be here tomorrow—why don't you consult him? He's a successful man of business.'

'Lucille, if he's following you here, it must be serious. Are you going to marry him?'

'He thinks so.'

'This isn't a time to be flippant, Lucille; this is not a thing to joke about. What is he like?'

'He's the pipe-and-tweed type. He ought to have been a country squire, with a gun and

98

retrievers and tenants pulling forelocks. When he's in town, he looks like what I said he was: a successful man of business.'

'You make me reassured. *Are* you going to marry him? I should so like to see you married. I know the last time—the first time—wasn't a success, but the years are going by, you know. Don't you want a nice, solid husband to take care of you?'

'Not much.'

'You don't sound in love—but you were always such an odd girl. I know that life with your father must have been difficult. His brother wasn't easy to live with, either—but one has to, as they say, make a go of it. I think I did.'

You certainly did, was Lucille's inward comment. She looked across at the mild, still-pretty face and decided that if at any time she had felt the urge to confide her love affairs to anybody, it would not have been to her aunt.

'Well, ask Malcolm about this venture of yours,' she persisted, and waited to see how Madame would get out of it.

'My dearest, if he's coming to see you, he won't want to be bothered with my little problems.'

'Not if he's going to be your nephew?'

'That would be all the more reason for being careful not to bore him. Besides which, I shall be going shortly after he arrives; that doesn't leave much time for discussion.'

'You ought to have someone to advise you.'

'That was what I thought. I was making myself ill worrying about what I should do. So I went and spoke to such a charming man—a Monsieur Ducros, who knows a great deal about properties of this kind. He was so kind! We spoke English, which was so helpful, as my French was sometimes not quite up to difficult business terms. He came down here to look at the property. He brought his fiancée with him—he's going to be married to an English girl. I can't say I cared for her; it seemed to me that he was throwing himself away—but *that*, naturally, didn't come into our little discussion. Shall we have coffee?'

'I'll bring it.'

They had coffee, and afterwards went down to the shop, where Lucille wrote down one or two points her aunt wished her to remember. Then, remembering that Malcolm would probably have lunch with them on the next day, she went out to buy food before the later-closing shops shut.

She had not far to go; everything she needed could be bought along the Rue des Dames. She took no money with her; the first year here had taught her that the accepted principles of paying back did not operate in her aunt's case; since then she had bought what was needed for the table, and charged the goods to Madame Camille. Madame Camille had made no comment; she took her few failures philosophically.

Lucille's French, in spite of a late start, was good; as she shopped, she found a slight rustiness falling away, leaving her fluent and at ease. She was greeted by old friends, but in each shop she entered, she sensed a kind of tension, and she realised that the news of her aunt's visit to old Madame Lachaise was known, and not approved of.

There was, as usual, a crowd of busy housewives at the épicerie; across their heads, Lucille saw Monsieur Didron's eyes fixed on her, and read in them a desire to say something to her. When his wife had served her, he carried the purchases into the street and drew her out of the way of passers-by.

'Mademoiselle,' he said without preamble, 'is it true that Madame your aunt is about to buy the Lachaise property? Forgive me; I have been waiting for you to come, to ask you.'

'I think, Monsieur, she has already bought it.'

'Ah! It is thought, here, that she had not yet made the final arrangements.'

'I don't know whether she has or not; I'm only going on the fact that she never speaks of a matter like this unless she's quite sure...'

'Yes, I see.'

'I shouldn't, perhaps, have told you; you'll understand that I'm speaking in confidence. But I remembered, when my aunt spoke of it, that you had once told me that your wife was related to Madame Lachaise and that you would have first chance of buying the shop if Monsieur Lachaise decided to retire. I don't mind other people not knowing about the matter, but I felt you'd prefer to be told the truth.'

'Mademoiselle, I am grateful; believe me. But I think that I knew the truth when I saw the lawyer, Ducros, going to see Madame; I know that property is his business.' He handed her the packages. 'Madame Camille,' he said, 'is a charming lady; it is a pity that charming ladies have to interest themselves in this kind of business. It is too late to say so, of course, but we here are almost all of the opinion that Madame Camille would have been wiser not to move. Her present shop suited her; it was small, pretty—like herself. Out there on the Avenue'—he spoke as if it were a thousand miles away—'out there, she will lose all this. Out there, it is difficult; it is impersonal. But I think that Madame knows what she is doing.'

Lucille, walking slowly homeward, thought so too. The mask would be allowed to slip. The move to the corner shop represented more than a desire for expansion; it was a change not only of business policy but of tactics. The long years of pretence, of cadging, of play-acting were at an end; Madame Camille, rich and successful but still ambitious, was on her way.

On the following morning, Madame went down to the shop while Lucille went to meet

Malcolm. She went with mixed feelings; she could not decide whether relief or apprehension was uppermost. She had had time to think, and had merely thought herself into a state more muddled than before. Now, she told herself desperately, she must pull herself together. Her own ingratitude appalled her; a good man loved her and wanted to marry her; he had spent the past two weeks buying a home for her. If she took a piece of paper and wrote down all the blessings which life was holding out within her reach, they would add up to a future which she would be crazy to refuse.

On paper...

If she didn't want to marry Malcolm, she asked herself, what did she want instead? She could not tell. Not the agency; she did not, like her aunt, want to expand. Was this lunatic hesitation caused by the fact that what they called true love was missing from this contract? What was true love? Wasn't it the accepted aspect of true love that had swept her into marriage with James Tandy? She had thought him the best, the finest as well as the most handsome man any girl had ever been lucky enough to meet; she had entrusted herself to him with a willingness which now seemed to her not only incredible but pathetic. She had also entrusted to him the few thousand pounds that had come to light unexpectedly on the death of her father. They had gone and he had gone, and one would think that the experience would have taught her to value a man as solid as Malcolm Donne. Instead of which she was staring at his descending plane and praying that he had missed it.

She might have known that he was a man who did not miss planes. Watching him when at last he came walking towards her, she was relieved to feel a sense of security creeping over her. He looked fit, reliable, clean-living, well-dressed, eminently presentable. She could not ask more.

It was comforting, after her experience of the Professor's uncouth ways, to find herself met with warmth, guided carefully past barriers, assisted tenderly into a taxi and studied with anxious care.

'Let me look at you,' Malcolm said. 'You're browner. And still beautiful.'

She was in his arms; the driver, sympathetic, slowed down and took the corners with less verve.

'I've missed you, Lucille. If I hadn't been so surrounded by agents and architects, I'd have risked my tyres on your Professor's road. Why didn't you send me a line?'

'I was working hard. How is your mother?'

'In her element. If this sale falls through, she'll be even more disappointed than I will.'

'There's a hitch?'

'Yes. An argument about boundaries. It'll be sorted out, I daresay; in the meantime, I took an architect up to the house to see what he thought of it. He thinks we ought to build on a bit at right-angles from the dining-room end—it would give a bit of shelter from the north-east. I've brought a couple of rough sketches to show you; it's no use doing anything more until this boundary dispute's cleared up. I had a survey done, of course; the report showed nothing wrong except a bit of damp in one of the attics. Very sound construction, they said—but I knew that already. My mother thinks we ought to change the rooms round—she thinks every drawing-room ought to face south and west, and every bedroom east; sensible enough; you get all the sun that's going. Pity the ground slopes so much in front; it makes my idea of a terrace pretty expensive.' He leaned back and frowned. 'Damned nuisance having to make all these plans merely provisionally.'

'But didn't you say the boundary dispute would be cleared up?'

'Well, yes—but there's always a chance that they're entitled to those two fields, and if they are, I'm not prepared to pay the price they're asking.'

'Do you want the two fields particularly?'

'I'm thinking of the principle of the thing. If you agree to a price, you're not going to pay it unless you get all you thought you were going to get. I'm keen on the place, but I can't stand being led by the nose. I've told them so and left them to think it over.'

'It's nice to see you. You must have had to get up very early to get that plane.'

'I was up at five. I've left the car at home; I hired a car to get to the airport. I'm thinking of hiring one here.'

'Is it worth it? My aunt's going away this evening; after that, I'm in charge. I'll have to be at the shop all day, every day.'

He turned to look at her.

'It's odd,' he said thoughtfully, 'that whenever you mention your aunt, you sound ... different. A bit sarcastic. Why is that? If you weren't fond of her, you wouldn't be here helping her out.'

She wondered what she would tell him—if she ever told him. If she could have been sure that he would regard the matter as she did—as a somewhat grim little comedy—she would not have hesitated to tell him the story. But he had prim patches; he also, while priding himself on being broad-minded and a good mixer, went to some pains to ensure that those he mixed with did not require him to exercise too much broad-mindedness. Her aunt as a little woman struggling along selling cosmetics was one thing; her aunt cadging and cheating was another. It was better to say nothing.

'What will you do all day?' she asked him.

'Oh, I've got a lot that'll fill in the time. A bit of business to do with the Cowleys, for a start—remember the Cowleys?'

'No.'

'I thought you met them at my mother's. Good bridge players. He's in wool. He's over here for a week or two, and promised to let me in on a shipment of wine.'

'Going to do any sight-seeing?'

'Not this trip. I've got a fairly long shopping list, though—mostly for my mother.'

He groped in his pockets to make sure he had brought it. She sat quietly, outwardly composed, inwardly at war with herself. But her interval at Hill House had, she realised, at least done one thing: it had made her see her problem more clearly. It had made her understand that if she married a man so settled, so sure of himself, so decisive, she would be bound to lead his life. She could be sure of it now, in the taxi, listening to his bald statements, his assured conclusions. She would not lead a life of her own; she would lead his life. Already she could—if she let herself go—be drawn along, carried along, borne on the fast-moving stream. It was like religion, she thought; once you could sweep aside all your doubts, once you could give yourself up, you had no further worry; the whole thing was taken care of. The whole thing went along, and you went with it. Malcolm would marry her, house her, take care of her, provide friends and amusements for her, horses and hobbies for her; he would plan trips, buy the tickets, secure the best cabins and see to all the tipping. She would be a part of his busy, well-organised existence. He did his duty as a son, as a householder, as a landowner, as a citizen; he would do it as husband and father. All she had to do was marry him and slip into her groove and the machinery would go on running smoothly.

'What are you thinking of?' he asked her smilingly.

'Lunch,' she lied, in order to avoid telling him that she was thinking of a man with a long, pointed nose who washed his own socks every night and hung them on the window-sill to dry.

'Where would you like to go and eat?'

'We're having lunch with my aunt.'

'I wasn't thinking of leaving her out.'

'It's a matter of time-tables. We've got to have a quick lunch and then I shall see her off at the station—you can go straight to your hotel, if you like.'

The taxi stopped before her aunt's shop. It was closed for lunch; Lucille led Malcolm up the narrow stairs that led from the street straight up to the flat. There was no sign of Madame Camille, but in the drawing-room were glasses and a tray of drinks—a courtesy she had never before extended to any friend of Lucille's.

Her suitcases had been put in the little hall downstairs; they had placed Malcolm's beside them and dismissed the taxi. When Madame Camille came out of her room, she was ready to travel—in a beautiful grey suit and a hat which she smilingly claimed to be one of Madame Baltard's—with the decorations severely pruned.

An introduction, a word or two, and it was clear that she and Malcolm were made for one another. Purring, Lucille noted without surprise. She looked on admiringly at the technique of male subjugation and marvelled at her aunt's superb performance. It was a pity she was thinking of leaving the stage.

Throughout lunch, Malcolm gave the two women his attention; after lunch he gave Madame Camille his assistance; he was full of solicitude and reminded her about passports, tickets, keys, wraps, as though she were bound for the South Pole instead of the south of France.

A taxi was called; the luggage was put in— Malcolm's too, as Lucille would be leaving him at the hotel on her way back to the shop. She and her aunt were settled on the seat facing the driver; Malcolm sat opposite.

'It's so sad to think that you won't be here when I come back,' Madame Camille told him. 'You must look after Lucille while I'm away.'

'I certainly will,' he promised.

'Has Lucille told you that I've taken a ... well, a plunge? I've decided to enlarge my little business. The shop next door—the one which has a window facing the Avenue—fell vacant, and I decided to buy it.'

109

So she had been right, Lucille thought. This was the first step into the open. None of the usual pretty little hesitations about risky ventures or mortgages. Perhaps her aunt was merely being tactful and presenting herself to her niece's fiancé as a woman of substance.

'Will you change your quarters too?' Malcolm asked.

'Oh no. I shall stay in my present flat. I shall let the one over the new shop. In fact, I've already done so.'

'I'm glad you're not moving,' Malcolm said. 'Your flat is charming. The new shop's bound to be a success. I admire your pluck—but who was it who said that if you don't speculate, you can't accumulate?'

'Solomon,' said Lucille, before she could check herself. 'When can we look at it?'

'Not just at present,' Madame said. 'A friend of mine has asked if he could put some things in the basement—just for a little while. Lucille'— the soft voice became crisper—'you will remember, won't you, not to give anybody credit? No credit whatsoever; for anybody. Do you understand?'

'Yes. Anything else?'

'I allow certain clients credit, but they must wait until I return; you wouldn't be able to remember who they were. And one thing more: Monsieur Ducros will call tonight—he is bringing round some papers. Please put them in the steel despatch box. You don't want to

110

ask me anything before I go?'

'No; I think I've got everything straight.'

'You'll hurry back to the shop, won't you?'

'Yes.'

'You've got my address and telephone number?'

'Yes.'

They reached the train with some difficulty; the train from Calais had just come in, and from its carriages streamed and apparently endless succession of late holiday-makers. English voices hailed French porters; Madame Camille, jostled and pushed, signalled to Lucille and Malcolm to leave her.

'You go; I'll follow you when I've put her on her train,' Malcolm said. 'Wait for me by the taxis.'

She stood by the taxi rank wondering whether she would be late at the shop. Turning for a moment, she saw with relief Malcolm making his way through the crowd; now she could see about getting a taxi. The porter in charge of Malcolm's luggage got one for her; over her shoulder she saw Malcolm almost beside her.

She moved forward and for an instant was halted by a porter with a selection of suitcases strapped about his person. At the same moment she felt a strong push that jerked her forward; she turned her head just in time to see the back of a man hurrying away—then Malcolm had caught her arm and was piloting her to the taxi.

'I wish I'd been nearer when that swine shoved you,' he said angrily. 'He was just out of reach. He was—'

He stopped abruptly and threw himself back on the cushions, out of sight of a woman who was making frantic signals from across the road.

'Tell the fellow to drive on,' he muttered. 'Quickly.'

'There's a woman making signs to you—do you know her?'

'No, I don't.' The taxi gathered speed and he sat forward and sighed with relief. 'She's a woman who sat next to me on the plane this morning and insisted on telling me her history. I had to put up with it on the journey, but I didn't want any more of it. That's why I hurried you into a taxi when I arrived.'

'She looked quite pretty. She could have helped you to—'

'She was an impossible woman. She told me some melodramatic tale about a fiancé of hers who let himself into the house when the family was away and stole some china. She's over here hunting for him. You don't think I want to get mixed up in that, do you? I asked her why she didn't let the police search for him—that led to even more sordid revelations about not being able to approach them because—well, to be frank, I did my best to keep my mind off what she was saying.'

Lucille stared at him, her mind going back to the paper on which the Professor's visitor had written her name and address.

'She isn't by any chance,' she asked, 'somebody called Clitheroe?'

Malcolm's face expressed open horror.

'You don't ... you don't mean you know her?' he asked in his turn.

'She came to see the Professor while I was working for him.'

'A friend of his?'

'No. Her fiancé—or ex-fiancé—had left the Professor's address lying about, and she came to see what the connection was. The Professor couldn't help her.'

'I can't help her either—and I don't want to be chased round Paris being asked to. Is this the hotel?' he asked, as the taxi stopped.

'Yes.'

She saw at once that it would not do; he did not care for it. She had chosen it not only because it was near the shop, but also because she liked its atmosphere and its proprietors. It was a family hotel; what Malcolm clearly objected to was the fact that the family was the proprietors'. He picked his way over babies and toddlers to the reception desk—a homely affair presided over by Grandmamma. She put aside her knitting to attend to him and summoned a six-year-old to take him up in the lift to his room. Lucille waited for him.

'I think, if you've no objection, I'll go

113

somewhere else tomorrow. This isn't quite my idea of comfort. Why do they allow those children to clutter up the public rooms?'

'Well, they live here. I mean, they're Madame's children.'

'But you can't expect guests to put up with them, however fond they are of children.'

'Why not move straight away?'

'Tomorrow. What time will you be free to come out and dine with me tonight?'

'Would eight be all right?'

'Eight would be splendid. I'll walk back to the shop with you now.'

'No—it's not worth it. Just see me out.'

They walked through the hall. Malcolm opened the double door that led to the avenue and stood aside to allow Lucille to pass. Instead, Miss Clitheroe entered.

She came in looking agitated, her head going from side to side as though in search of someone—and then she saw Malcolm.

'Oh, Mr Donne!' It was a prayer of thankfulness. 'Oh, I'm so glad I've found you! I thought we'd missed you. I told the taxi man to follow your taxi, but he wasn't sure this was where you stopped.'

'Ah,' Malcolm said. 'Well, I'm so sorry. As you see, I'm just going out.'

'Are you staying here?' she asked. 'I mean, I haven't fixed up anything yet. Couldn't I—'

'I don't recommend this place.' Malcolm's words, spoken too loudly, brought many heads

114

round to gaze at him, and the knowledge that he was being made conspicuous brought the angry colour to his cheeks. 'And now if you'll excuse me—'

Lucille wondered how she could have thought the girl pretty—but watching her, she began to see that perhaps, after all, she had been right. At close range, the effect was one of mournfulness—large brown eyes, spaniel-like; a long face, a drooping mouth. It added up to something like beauty—she looked like an elongated Madonna. She also looked as though she wanted to cling to Malcolm's arm.

'You were so kind on the plane,' she said. 'I thought—'

Lucille glanced at Malcolm's angry face and heard herself speaking.

'Haven't you registered anywhere yet?' she asked.

The girl turned to her gratefully.

'No. I only heard from the detectives last night—they said if I wanted to catch the man, he was on the train that would arrive in Paris this afternoon. So I took the first plane and went to the station, but I missed him. I waited where I could see all the passengers coming out, and then I saw him. He was the man who pushed you. I screamed at him, but naturally he wasn't going to wait. He disappeared. So now'—she turned once more to Malcolm—'so now what do I do?'

Her voice had risen to a wail. Everybody

115

within hearing distance had given up the pretence of lack of interest; they were drinking in every word. Malcolm's face had gone from red to white; he looked hunted. His eyes met Lucille's with something between an appeal and a command: *Get her away from here.*

'Where's your luggage?' Lucille asked her.

'Outside in the taxi.'

'Malcolm, will you have it brought in? Miss Clitheroe can stay here, if Madame has a room.'

Madame had a room. Everybody looked relieved; act two, with luck, would be played on the premises.

'Did Mr Donne tell you my name?'

'No. I was working for Professor Hallam when you went to see him. You wrote down your name and address and I saw it.'

'You were there? At the Professor's?' Miss Clitheroe's voice rose to a squeak. 'Why, it was the Professor who gave me the idea of private detectives! I said I had to keep the police out of it, and he—'

'Would you very kindly lower your voice?' Malcolm asked in a low, furious tone. 'As you see, we are surrounded by gaping spectators.'

'I work in a shop just round the corner,' Lucille said. 'If you'd like to walk round this evening, Miss Clitheroe, I—'

'Oh please, *please* will you call me Barbara? I hate being Miss Clitheroe. You too,' she invited Malcolm. 'I'll go to the shop this

116

evening. I've never been on my own before in a place where I can't speak the language, and it makes me panicky. When Mr Donne was so kind on the plane, it seemed like a sort of miracle.'

Lucille left them—Malcolm and Miss Clitheroe and the listeners. She walked to the shop feeling that Malcolm had not come well out of the affair. Even before the advent of Barbara Clitheroe, she had been aware of something new in his manner: something that came near to heartiness. She came to the surprised conclusion that he did not transplant well. She was also amazed at his self-consciousness—but there, perhaps, she was judging him too harshly; most men would have been embarrassed at being trapped in Miss Clitheroe's company.

She opened the shop and went thoughtfully inside. Miss Clitheroe was in Paris looking for her china. Monsieur Reynaud was, or had been in Canterbury, looking for his pictures. There seemed no possible connection between the two ... and yet there was a thread linking them. Not a thread; a piece of paper. A piece of paper torn off the top of a letter. A piece of paper with the Professor's address printed on it.

CHAPTER FIVE

Miss Clitheroe arrived just as the shop closed—so promptly, that Lucille wondered how long she had been hovering. She looked pale and depressed; up in the flat, she broke into noisy weeping.

'I know he thinks I'm being a nuisance,' she sobbed. 'But he was so nice to me on the plane.'

'Mr Donne?'

'Yes. He told me he's engaged to you. Can I call you Lucille?'

'Please do. And please don't cry; you're probably tired out, but there's nothing else to cry for.'

'Didn't you know that all our valuable china had been stolen? It's worth at least—'

'You'll probably get it back; these detectives seem to be on the trail. I hope they find him— that was a vicious push he gave me.'

'He must have seen me just before I saw him—and now he's g-got away and where does that l-leave me?'

'Well, dry your eyes and let's find out,' Lucille said. 'Would you like a drink?'

'A strong one,' Barbara said, visibly cheered.

Lucille opened her aunt's cabinet and poured out two drinks. She would have to be careful to replace what she took.

'Drink that up,' she said, handing a glass to Barbara. 'And then, if you'll take my advice, you'll go back to the hotel, have a nice hot bath, get into bed and make them send you up dinner. Madame's a motherly soul; she'll look after you.'

'I can't understand a single word she says.'

'I thought everybody could speak some sort of French.'

'Everybody but me. I was terrified of coming over here alone, but I was more terrified of my mother coming back from her cruise and finding the china gone.'

'She doesn't know?'

'No.'

'Why not tell her?'

'She'll want to know why it was so easy to get into the house. When she finds out it was with my key, she'll jump to a lot of conclusions.'

'Correct ones?'

'Yes.' The tears began to flow once more. 'So you see how t-terrible it all is?'

'Are you frightened of your mother?'

Barbara stopped crying in order to stare in astonishment.

'Frightened? No. She's strait-laced, that's all. You wouldn't believe how narrow she is. Her family were all very religious. They all grew out of it—I mean, they got to be more reasonable—but not my mother. She stayed strait-laced. If she knew about the key, she could make it awkward for me. If she knew I'd

119

let my fiancé stay in the house once or twice when she was away, she'd stop giving me money. I've got money of my own, but not enough to live the way I live. With what she gives me. I can live my own life. I live with her, but not *with* her, if you follow me; I'm free to do nearly all I want to do. All that would stop if she started asking questions about keys and things. So my only hope is to find out where the china is, and make a deal.'

Lucille leaned back in her chair and tried to imagine herself relating intimate family details to a complete stranger. She was beginning to understand, however, that this girl would talk to anybody who would listen; deprived of someone in whom she could confide, she felt lost. She had been preparing to cling to Malcolm; now she was happy to feel that Lucille would do something to help her. Uneasily, Lucille remembered her dinner engagement and wondered how difficult it was going to be to disengage herself.

It proved impossible. Hints, a removal of herself to have a bath and change, a refusal to offer another drink—none of these had any effect. When Malcolm rang the bell, she had to go down and, by signs, tell him that Miss Clitheroe was still present.

'Is that Malcolm?' Barbara called from above.

'Yes. Good evening.'

'I was wondering if you'd both come and

dine with me. You've been so kind, and I can't bear dining alone.'

'You're going home to get into bed and have a nice light dinner sent up to you,' Lucille told her firmly. 'Malcolm, call a taxi and put Miss Clitheroe into it.'

Thankfully, gratefully, he went with great strides to the corner and returned hanging on to the door of a taxi. Barbara, tearful but resigned, was put into it and sent away.

'That was well done,' he said, following Lucille up the stairs. 'I'm going to move first thing tomorrow, before she's down. Is there a drink I could have?'

'Help yourself; it's all my aunt's.'

'I'll get in a stock. Where are we dining?'

It was a question she felt unnecessary and irritating; if he was taking her out, he ought to decide where. And if he didn't, the thing to do was to lead him to the most expensive restaurant in the district, order whatever cost the most and thus teach him to arrive with his plans already made.

'The *Richelieu's* nice,' she said. 'Let's go there.'

He was not, he said angrily, when they were seated side by side on a brocaded bench, dressed for a place like this.

'You know quite well that I like to be changed when I come to a place of this kind,' he told her.

'You'll be charged instead of changed.

121

Relax; the food's wonderful. They have a very good pâté and they've got a special way of doing lobsters.'

'You're in an expensive mood, aren't you?'

'Aren't you?'

'Who brings you to these pricey places?'

'My aunt has admirers. She ... Malcolm, *look* at that woman's dress; isn't it gorgeous?'

He thought it was too décolleté. He was not happy; they were surrounded by the smart, and he was annoyed at looking—he said—like a tourist.

'Tell me about the house,' she invited.

It proved successful as a diversion, but it brought him to the subject she was dreading: their engagement.

'My mother wants to know how you'd like the announcement worded,' he said.

'Miss Lucille Abbey—would you like me to be Miss, or shall I go on being Mrs? Mrs Lucille Abbey announces that she will probably marry Mr Donne, but has some reservations which she feels he ought to give his attention to.'

'Reservations—still?'

She stared at him for a few moments.

'Am I really,' she asked slowly, 'the kind of woman you want to marry?'

'Since you've asked for it,' he said, 'no. You're not. I didn't think I'd marry at all; if I did, I thought it would certainly be a girl out of my own set—one of the girls I'd known for years, taken out, danced with, hunted with,

122

played golf and tennis with. Never did I imagine falling in love with a woman who never got out of town suits, town dresses and high heels. But it happened. I fell in love with you.'

'And you're sure it'll work out?'

'I'm sure. My mother isn't.'

'Do you care about what she thinks—in this matter?'

'Of course I do. She knows me better than anybody does. She knows what I am, what I need, how I'll react. She thinks you won't try to fit in. She thinks you'll expect me to change—and of course, I won't. I'm too settled, too old to change.'

'Wouldn't things work out better if you kept on your office? For a time, I mean.'

'No. I've had enough of keeping a foot in each place—town and country. I wanted to make some more money; I've made it. Now I want to get out—get back to where I came from: the land. It isn't as though I'm condemning you to a primitive existence miles from anywhere. It isn't—'

He stopped abruptly; she had given a cry of dismay.

'What's the matter?' he asked.

'Monsieur Ducros.'

'Monsieur *who*?'

'Don't you remember? My aunt said that her lawyer, Monsieur Ducros, was coming tonight and bringing some papers. They're probably the papers—'

'He can bring them tomorrow night, can't he?'

'We ought to have had dinner at the flat. I could have cooked you an omelette and—'

'Thank you very much—but on my first night with you, I consider I've slightly more right to your company than this Ducros.'

'He's probably coming all the way out from his office—'

'Are you expected to work out of hours?'

'No. I'm just sorry that I forgot he was coming, that's all.'

'And I'm just sorry that you can break into a discussion which affects our whole future, to drag in some French lawyer. You do it over and over again. You do it all the time. Sometimes I have the feeling that you never really listen when I'm talking.'

'I *was* listening. But you heard my aunt—'

'There's no need to raise your voice.'

'I didn't. It's just that you can't bear anybody to look at you.'

'If you mean I dislike being the target of amused glances, you're right. I'm only surprised you didn't land me with dinner for three—us and the Clitheroe.'

'Don't let's quarrel. Not on your first night here. How long are you going to stay?'

'That depends on you. My idea was to come over, stay a few days, fix up our engagement and go back to announce it—but nothing ever

124

works out quite so simply when one's dealing with you. You've either got a peculiarly elusive quality, or you don't want to be pinned down. My mother is of the opinion that you don't want to be pinned down.'

'Couldn't your mother's name be—'

'Kept out of it? No. She doesn't interfere, but I'm quite prepared to take her advice on most matters.'

There was silence. The soft mood that was beginning to surround them was shattered. He was angry, and she wished they had stayed at home.

The remainder of the meal was eaten for the most part in silence. Lucille, thinking of Monsieur Ducros, did her best to appear unhurried, but she knew that she was growing impatient. They had dined early; if they went back now, there was still a chance that they would not miss him. She did not think the matter so important, but her business sense was offended at the idea of a man going out of his way to deliver some papers, and finding the door bolted and barred.

In the taxi, he took her fiercely in his arms; he seemed to her to be trying to make her feel his strength, his determination to keep matters in his own hands and bring them to a successful termination. She tried to respond; perhaps if there had been less anger, more tenderness in his embrace she would have felt stirred. As it was, her mind refused to close, to blot out all

125

thoughts but the present; glimpses, memories came more and more insistently: cold air and a warm stove and refuge at the top of a high hill.

She was glad when he released her. She was glad when he refused to come up to the flat; she was glad when he drove away.

She went upstairs, opened a window and stood looking out. It was cold; she drew her coat more closely round her. Down in the little street all was quiet; lights showed here and there in the houses, but shutters were closed, nobody was out under the trees. She felt tears stinging her eyes, but she did not let them fall. Crying was no use. All she had to do was think. She had no right to keep him hanging about; she either wanted him or she didn't; she must make up her mind.

But not tonight. She was tired and she was depressed. She closed the window and walked into her bedroom.

The bell rang just as she had begun to undress. For a moment she wondered whether Malcolm had come back; he had a way of returning if they had parted on a sour note. But as she went downstairs, she remembered Monsieur Ducros.

When she opened the door, she saw a short, smiling, good-looking man.

'Meeses Abbey? I am—'

'You're Monsieur Ducros.'

'Yes. I am sorry to be late; I could not get here before. I have brought some papers—

your aunt will have told you that I was coming.'

'Yes. Thank you very much.'

She took the long, bulky envelope. Glancing past him, she saw a car whose engine seemed to be twice as long as the seating accommodation. From its open window a girl looked out at Lucille. She was dark, with a rather square face; she had a blunt nose and a large mouth. Her hair was a frank, fashionable wig; a diamond bracelet gleamed on a bare arm. Her expression was bored, but as she stared across at Lucille, a frown appeared on her forehead.

'Hey,' she called. 'I know you.'

Something in the loud, assured voice stirred Lucille's memory. She saw the girl, with a sudden movement, open the car door and step out—a beautiful figure, beautifully dressed.

'This is my fiancée,' said Monsieur Ducros. 'Miss Bannerman.'

'I heard the name Abbey, but it didn't register,' Miss Bannerman said. 'But you once ran a secretarial agency in London.'

'I still do.'

'Well, you interviewed me once—remember?'

All at once, Lucille remembered clearly.

'Yes. I—'

'You turned me down. I never understood why. Now you can tell me—but not in front of François. Didn't you trust me with all those dirty old business magnates?'

127

'Do we,' Monsieur Ducros asked mildly, 'have to discuss this on a doorstep? We are going to dine—if Mrs Abbey has not already dined, why doesn't she come too?'

'What—with all your dreary sisters and cousins and aunts? Are you crazy?' screamed his fiancée. 'Why don't we go on up and have a drink? I want to have a good, long talk with Mrs Abbey.'

'My dear Diana, we are already late.'

'Then you go ahead and tell them my suspender broke. I'll follow you in a taxi and be there before you're through the first helping of snails.'

He laughed good-humouredly.

'They are coming especially to meet her,' he explained to Lucille. 'She came over to Paris to meet them all, and then she—'

'That wasn't the only reason, and you know it,' interrupted his fiancée. 'Oh go on, François—be a devil; walk in and tell them I overslept with your rival.'

He took her arm and turned her firmly towards the car.

'You are coming with me, ma belle. You shall come here tomorrow and unveil the past with Mrs Abbey.'

'When can we meet?' shouted Miss Bannerman, from inside the car. 'Are you free for lunch tomorrow?'

'I—'

'Put them off. I'll call for you. 'Bye.'

128

The car streaked away. Lucille went upstairs smiling, recalling the interview that had taken place in her office. Miss Bannerman had struck her as somewhat too flamboyant for a sober secretarial job, so she had not engaged her, but she had enjoyed her uninhibited comments, her loud but invigorating laugh and her light-hearted view of life. She would not be able to accept the invitation for lunch tomorrow; Malcolm would be round as soon as the shop closed, and after tonight's unsatisfactory meal she owed him a conciliatory hour, with no strangers to spoil it. A sense of guilt weighed her down; his visit, she thought, had begun badly, and things were not going to get better.

She went to bed filled with doubts and woke feeling tired, but once she was installed behind the gleaming counter, she forgot everything but the work in hand: face creams, lotions, powders in little boxes to offer, prices to be checked and spot cash insisted on. There was slight trouble over this last, two women insisting that Madame Camille had always—*mais toujours, toujours*—made the little arrangement. The little arrangement, Lucille explained firmly, was suspended until Madame's return.

As she expected, Malcolm was waiting when she closed the shop for lunch. They went up the stairs together, and he caught her hand as they reached the top, and drew her to him.

'Next time you want to spoil my dinner,' he

said, 'choose a less expensive restaurant.'

'I'm sorry. I'm sorry for everything. Sit down and I'll bring you a drink.'

'I didn't come to sit down. I've come to take you out—and without delay, because although I bribed the proprietress heavily to persuade the Clitheroe to have a morning in bed and lunch sent up to her, I have a feeling she'll appear at any moment.'

'When are you moving out of the hotel?'

'Tomorrow. I meant to go today, but Cowley's looked me out a place and there isn't a room free until tomorrow. It's nice to be near you, but I must admit to a liking for a bit more comfort than I'm getting round the corner. Are you ready to go?'

'Yes.'

'Then come on—but kiss me first.' He drew her towards him, pausing as the doorbell rang. 'Who the hell's that? That Clitheroe woman, for a certainty. You must get rid of her, Lucille.'

'It's not Miss Clitheroe.' Lucille guessed who was making the door resound with bangs and the bell sound without ceasing. 'It's a Miss Bannerman. Coming, coming, coming!' she shouted, to still the clamour.

'Who's Miss Bannerman?'

'I don't know her. She's going to marry my aunt's lawyer. She asked me out to lunch, and didn't wait to hear me say I couldn't go.'

'Hey, Lucille!' shouted Miss Bannerman,

130

banging anew upon the panels. 'Come on down, I'm thirsty!'

'Coming! I'm sorry, Malcolm. I'll tell her we're just going out to lunch.'

'Make certain she doesn't tag along. With her and that Clitheroe, we could have had a nice, cosy foursome.'

'Don't sound so annoyed. I tried to put her off.'

'You'll have to try harder. Damn it all, Lucille, I didn't come to Paris to get landed with a string of women you can't shake off.'

'Don't lose your temper. I couldn't help getting landed with Miss Clitheroe. She was clinging to you, not to me. And this Miss Bannerman is the type who doesn't wait for you to think of a polite excuse.'

Malcolm followed her downstairs.

'Leave me out of this,' he said. 'I really can't face getting entangled with yet another stray woman—especially one who sounds like this.'

Lucille opened the door. Outside was Diana Bannerman, radiating energy and joy-of-living. She was dressed in a green suit and exuded an exotic scent. Her make-up was too strong, today's wig was too red; the overall effect was overpowering.

'Well, well, well,' she shouted. 'Better late than never. I thought your bell must be out of order. Who's this?' she asked, indicating Malcolm. 'We taking him along?'

'You are not,' Malcolm said firmly, eyeing

131

her with cold dislike. 'You must excuse me. I have an appointment for lunch.'

Lucille was glad to hear it; she had entertained no hopes of getting rid of Miss Bannerman.

'Well, I don't mind giving you a lift,' Miss Bannerman told him. 'But you'll have to sit at the back. I wouldn't ask any woman to crawl in there and ruin her clothes. This is a hired car; François won't let me drive his, the mistrustful pig. Let's go.'

'You're very kind,' Malcolm said in a voice that would have left icicles on his moustache, if he had had one. 'I would rather walk.'

'Oh, go on!' Miss Bannerman said, giving him a strong push towards the car. 'You're frightened just because I said I give François nervous prostration. He's just a cowering Frenchie; you're a great big English hero, anybody can see that. Get in, get in, get *in* and relax. I've been driving since I was seventeen and I've only had five summonses.'

She had turned Malcolm round and was urging him, squeezing him into the inadequate space at the back of the car. She was not a small woman, and she looked as though she had been a member of her school hockey team; for all Malcolm's struggles, he was being forced inside. Lucille, cold with horror, could see only his broad haunches and his feebly-kicking feet.

'English tailoring,' Miss Bannerman said, of his impeccable trousers. 'You can always tell.

Go on, man—*shove*, can't you? That's it. Now you're in. Come on, Lucille.'

Lucille, averting her eyes from Malcolm's purple face and furious, starting eyes, got in.

'You didn't tell me his name,' Miss Bannerman reminded her.

'Mr Donne. Miss Bannerman,' Lucille said faintly.

No acknowledgement whatever came from behind, but this was perhaps because the car was proceeding briskly on the English side of the road. In answer to a sound between a groan and a gasp from the rear passenger, Miss Bannerman made a violent swerve to the right.

'Hell, I always forget,' she said irritably. 'Why can't they drive on the same side as we do? You two known each other long?'

'About two years,' said Lucille.

'Well, you can find out a lot in that time. I only met François four months ago, but with me, it's always quick; one look at him, and I knew I was his. So I promised to marry him, and never gave a thought to having to live in Paris for the rest of my life. It might turn out all right; after all, I love food and I love wine, wine, wine. Did you say last night that you were still running that agency? If you are, what're you doing in that powder-and-pomade shop?'

'I come over every year to take charge for my aunt while she takes a holiday.'

'Can't she afford an assistant? She can't be

133

hard up; I know what they were asking for that shop on the corner, and she bought it outright. I'm supposed to be getting married on the twenty-fifth; if you're back in London, you must come. Does anybody know where we are?'

'Place du Trocadero,' Lucille told her.

'Where's that?'

'You've just passed the Palais de Chaillot.'

'Well, that doesn't help. François said that if I kept going after coming out of your street, I'd come to a restaurant called the Three Bears in French. Would that one over there be it?'

'Look out!' came from Malcolm in a choked voice. 'My God, that was a close thing!'

'It would have been his fault,' said Miss Bannerman. 'How can I look for three bears and see him coming at the same time?'

'There it is—*Trois Ours*,' Lucille said.

'Can I turn here?'

She could and did; it involved a complete hold-up of traffic coming from every direction. To the accompaniment of brakes screaming on all sides, she drew up outside the restaurant and leaned out to wave a note at the approaching doorman—a uniformed and imposing figure.

'Look, Buttons,' she told him, 'you park this car for me, hm? When we've eaten, you can fetch it back for me.'

She and Lucille got out. With the doorman's help, they extricated Malcolm. He said

134

nothing; standing on the pavement, pale and tight-lipped, he gave himself to the rearrangement of his clothes.

'You look fine,' Miss Bannerman assured him. 'What's a crease here and there? Come on in. Lunch is on me.'

'I'll say goodbye,' Malcolm said, addressing himself pointedly and frigidly to Lucille. 'Ring me up when you're free, will you?'

'Can't we all meet for dinner somewhere?' Miss Bannerman suggested. 'You can't think how nice it is for me to have a change from François' *oncle* and *tante* and rather frightful *mère*. It's a shame not to see something of you, now that we've met. How about tonight?'

'Thank you. *No.*' Malcolm said, in a voice of granite.

'He doesn't want to; you can see that,' Miss Bannerman said without resentment. 'Well, Lucille, why not leave him out and meet me somewhere? Or is he on your hands?'

'I am not,' Malcolm said slowly and clearly, 'on anybody's hands.'

'Now, don't get huffy, Mr ... what did you say your name was?'

Without answering, Malcolm, having raised his hat and then clamped it firmly on his head, turned on his heel and strode away. Miss Bannerman looked after him with raised eyebrows, and then took Lucille's arm and led her into the restaurant.

'Touchy type,' she commented. 'Before you

get too deep, I'd do something about that parade-ground manner of his.'

They went inside and Miss Bannerman bribed a barman to arrange a table; then they sat down and ordered drinks.

'You must look nice in that cosmetic shop,' Miss Bannerman said, leaning back and surveying Lucille. 'You've got that sort of gorgeous skin. Anything serious between you and that Donne?'

'We're on the point of getting engaged—I think,' Lucille added, recalling Malcolm's expression as he took his departure.

'Then I'd think again. I grant you he's handsome, but that perfect-English-little-gentleman type's a bit of an old model, don't you agree? I can't see him making anybody nice and warm in bed—and isn't that one thing you need in a man? Mind you, I'm not running him down; I'm just warning you. Tell me why you didn't give me that job I went after. Didn't you like me?'

'They showed me the typing test you'd done.'

'I might have improved in time.'

'You didn't look as though you needed a secretarial job—and you didn't look as though you'd keep it for long if you got one.'

'Well, I've never been poor and needy—but every now and then I used to get a sort of urge to support myself all alone, like other women, in a nice, steady job. So I used to go out looking for a nice, steady job, and nobody ever gave me one.'

She led the way to their corner table and sat looking disparagingly round at the other lunchers.

'Lousy with François' relations,' she reported. 'No wonder he told me to come here.'

'That's what you're in Paris for, isn't it—to meet them?'

'Yes. It seemed a good idea at the time, but it's gone sour on me. After being handed round his family, I feel as though I've had all my feathers plucked off. I feel lost. When François took you those papers last night and I looked out of the car and saw you, I thought you'd dropped straight down from heaven. I love François, but I wish he'd come and live in London. Between you and me, I never caught this spring-in-Paris mood. Paris always looked to me just like any other city. You can't say that out loud, of course; I don't. You have to know a few facts—historical facts—before you can get much value out of a city like Paris. Do you like what you're eating?'

'It's delicious. It's absolutely perfect.'

'So's mine. If a Frenchman wants to eat well, he knows where to go. I like Frenchman. It's funny; I was sure that if I ever got round to making up my mind to marry, I'd pick a Frenchman—and I have. Not that I'm good at choosing. The only time—except this time— that I got close to marrying, it was with a crook.'

'Are you serious?'

'Of course I'm serious. He went off with my jewels. He couldn't touch my money; he tried, but it was all tied up so tight that he couldn't put a finger on it. It's guarded by a trio of whiskery old trustees who dole it out together with long lectures on not spending it so fast. But the jewels were something else.'

'He *stole* them?'

'Nothing as crude as that. He simply went through them piece by precious piece, substituting fake stones for real ones. Then he left for good, leaving not a sign—not even a tail feather. The only piece I really shed tears over—because I loved it—was my little seahorse. He might have spared me that. It wasn't worth dismantling; its body was made of masses of seed pearls. I still miss it, after all this time—nearly three years. It had little ruby eyes and three little wavy turquoise lines under it to represent ocean waves. Sounds a mess, but it was beautiful, and I've never seen another like it anywhere. Why haven't you married again? You've waited a long time to pick out this— what's his name again?—Donne. You know what his trouble is? He's out of date. Take those clothes of his, for a start—pure London stockbroker. I'll bet that's what he is—right? I thought so. He's not on the job now—why can't he wear casual clothes, like everybody else on holiday?'

138

'Why should he go round in a flowered shirt and slacks if he doesn't want to?'

'Because it might unstiffen him a bit. He looks down his nose. Somebody ought to tell him—you, for instance—that people don't pull their forelocks any more. And somebody ought to tell you—me, for instance—that when a man of his type sets, he sets hard. Don't you want coffee?'

'No, thanks. I'll have to get back to the shop.'

'How about coming out and dining with François and me tonight?'

'I think I'd better keep the evening for Malcolm. Thanks all the same. And thanks for the nice lunch.'

'If you're decent enough to listen to me talking, and kind enough to keep me company, the least I can do is feed you. I'll drive you back.'

'No. Stay and finish your coffee.'

She went back alone. The afternoon in the shop seemed to pass quickly; she was surprised, glancing at her watch, to see that it was almost closing time. There was nobody in the shop; with luck, no more customers would come in and she would be able to close punctually. It was pouring with rain; she hoped there would be no customers of the kind who came in solely for shelter.

And then, when she had begun to think that it would be safe to begin covering the shelves, a woman came in.

English, she saw at once. Large, elderly, florid, rather motherly. Her shoes were sensible and she was enveloped in a damp mackintosh, but on her head, unmistakably, regrettably, was a hat that could have come only from Madame Baltard's. It looked wildly unsuitable on the grey head—but perhaps it was, after all, suited to a day like this, for posed round the crown were three or four little yellow ducks. Below the hat was an expression of growing consternation.

'Dear me! Madame Camille *est* ill? *Malade?*'

'Madame is away on holiday,' Lucille explained.

'Oh, you're English! Thank *goodness*. My French is really dreadful. I'm so sorry to have missed her. What a disappointment! And I had timed my visit rather carefully in the hope that if she had no engagement, she would come out and have a little dinner somewhere. I should never have the courage to go alone. I kept the taxi, just in case she could come.'

'I'm afraid she won't be back for two weeks.'

'That's a pity—I brought her a little present. She has been so kind to me; I can't *tell* you how kind. Are you related to her?'

'I'm her niece.'

'Then I don't have to tell you how good and charming she is. Did she mention that she had let the flat above the shop next door?'

'Yes; she did say something about it.'

140

'I wanted to bring her some little thing that would give her pleasure.' She placed a square, flat package on the counter. 'Could you perhaps put this where she would find it? I mean, would you put it in her room? I'll write her a little note and send it here by post. And now I must go or the taxi man will get fidgety. Oh dear me, dear me, you must be waiting to close the shop; I'm afraid I've delayed you...'

It was only a step to the taxi, but it was necessary to offer to hold an umbrella over Madame Baltard's hat; everyone knew what they cost. Lucille walked outside and opened the taxi door and settled the passenger inside. Then she walked back to the shop and did the extra tidying-up that was necessary on Saturday nights; Sunday and Monday were holidays.

Everything done, she picked up her aunt's present and went up to the flat. She eyed the telephone thoughtfully; Malcolm had told her to ring him up when she was free; angry and humiliated as he had been after his encounter with Diana Bannerman, it was not likely that he would make the first move towards conciliation.

She had not made up her mind when she heard the door bell. She went downstairs to answer it; she had no doubt that this would be Malcolm himself coming to take her out to dinner and restore harmonious relations. She was surprised, and a little moved; he had strong views about keeping his dignity and when he walked away from the restaurant he had been a very angry man indeed.

But it was not Malcolm she saw when she opened the door. Outside, standing in front of the beautiful car and the sulky chauffeur, was Monsieur Reynaud.

'Good evening, Lucille.'

He sounded far from friendly. Recovering from her surprise, she noted that though his grooming was as impeccable as ever, his manner had undergone a change. He was no longer debonair. He looked tired and irritable.

She took him upstairs and indicated a chair.

'Do sit down,' she invited. 'Have you—'

'You must know, my dear Lucille, why I am here,' he broke in. 'I find it interesting that you and I were together when I began my search; now we are together when it is ended. All I ask now is that you do not pretend to me. I am a little tired—too tired for children's games. I am tired of being a detective. I am tired of following old women. I am tired of ... well, just let us say that I am tired. All I ask now of you is the address.'

She stared at him blankly.

'What address?'

He sighed; it was a sound of exasperation.

'What address? Mrs Westover's address.'

'I haven't the faintest idea,' she said. 'But you knew. You went to Canterbury to—'

'Are you also going to tell me that you do not

know, you have not met, you have not seen Mrs Westover?'

'Of course I don't know her. I never set eyes on her in my life.'

'Ah. So it was a perfect stranger you accompanied to the taxi just now, and assisted with such solicitude?'

'Just now ... You mean just before I closed the shop?'

'Just before you closed the shop. Yes, that is what I mean.'

'That was ... was that ... Mrs Westover?'

He sighed again, more deeply.

'You are making it very difficult for me,' he said. 'I do not like to call you a liar. I do not even think that you are a liar. But if you are not, then what am I to think? She was here. Unfortunately, I did not see her go in; my car came up the street just as she came out of your aunt's shop. I did not stop; I thought I could follow her—but on the corner, the car was held up and the taxi went out of sight. So I came back, and now I am here and you deny that you know anything of Mrs Westover. If this is true, why was she with you?'

'She came into the shop just before it closed. She wanted to see my aunt, Madame Camille. I explained that she was away. She wanted to leave a present for her.'

'A present? Perhaps a picture?'

'No. There it is, over there. It's just a small package. She left it with me and asked me to

143

give it to my aunt when she returned. And then she went away in the taxi—and that was all. Except...'

'Except what?'

'My aunt has bought the shop next door—the one on the corner. She told me she'd let the flat above it, but she didn't say who was taking it. Mrs Westover mentioned it—but I didn't ask her if she was going to live in it.'

'She is not. Her niece is going to live in it. Her niece is getting married. She—'

'Look, can't we sit down and talk comfortably? You were angry when you came here, but you must believe by now that I don't know any more about Mrs Westover than I did when I was at the Professor's house. If you sit down, I can offer you a drink and—'

He sat down.

'You have cognac?' he enquired.

She hesitated. Her aunt had cognac—excellent cognac. It was kept apart, for special occasions or for illness.

'Yes,' she said.

'You are very kind. This is what I need. I did not know, until this past week, how old I was. I imagined that I was a man well-preserved, in some lights to be mistaken for thirty-five. I am disillusioned.'

She took a chair opposite to him.

'Could you tell me, from the beginning, what happened to you?'

'By the beginning, you mean from the time I

144

left the Professor's house?'

'Yes.'

'I left thankfully. I did not like the Professor. I was angry to have wasted so much time for nothing. With the address of Mrs Westover, I was satisfied that I could from now manage things in my own way. So I went to Canterbury. I went to the apartment house in which Mrs Westover lives. I asked for her, I was shown up to her apartment; I met her. Very politely, I explained that I had come from the house of Professor Hallam; I was interested in his mother's pictures, which I understood to be in her possession; would she be interested to sell them to me? And then...'

'And then?'

'May I, perhaps, ask for more of this magnificent cognac?'

'Of course.'

When he took up the tale again, his voice was puzzled.

'I would have said that I am a good judge of people—but this was another illusion. I said to myself that Mrs Westover was a stupid but honest woman; it was impossible for me to imagine her taking every one of her employer's pictures off the walls, packing them and running away with them. To my question, she answered—with a surprise that seemed genuine—that she had only one or two pictures painted by the late Mrs Hallam. She showed them to me. She seemed astonished when I told her that there were no pictures now hanging on the walls. She had left them there—she said. She had locked the rooms up, as the Professor had directed. She had come to live, not with her niece, but alone; she had lived formerly with her niece, but her niece had gone to Paris and was shortly going to be married there. And that was all. And perhaps I made a mistake when I showed her that I thought she had the pictures. Certainly I made a mistake when I said that I would give her a little time to think about my offer to buy them—a tempting offer. Above all I made a mistake in not realising that she might not, after all, be so honest as she appeared. For when I went back, she had gone. The apartment was closed. She had left for Paris—and if anybody knew the address of her niece, it was certain that they were not going to give it to me. There was only one clue: her niece was, or had been, an art student and had studied in Paris at the Beauvoir school. I came back to Paris; I enquired at the Beauvoir school if a Miss Westover had been there—for I did not know whether her name would be the same as her aunt's. They knew her. They gave me her address. I went there, to find Mrs Westover herself getting into a taxi. The taxi came, eventually, into this street—I do not know what it is called. We were some distance behind, but we had not lost the taxi. And the rest you know. And I am very tired. I thought that it was only in films that cars chase one

146

another along busy streets. It is very difficult and very dangerous. My chauffeur is going to leave me. But I am in Paris; I have been to my gallery and my assistant has shown me that he has done well in my absence. I am here; Mrs Westover is here; it is only reasonable to suppose that it is not her, but her niece, who will occupy your aunt's apartment. My next visit—but not tonight, perhaps not even tomorrow, for I am exhausted—will be to the niece. I think I can see some connection between the pictures and a niece who is an art student. Since I have played the detective, I can say that the net is closing. Mrs Westover ran away, proving that she knows something she did not care to tell me. Perhaps I shall find it out from the niece.'

He rose reluctantly; he had looked, for the past few minutes, comfortable and relaxed.

'Lucille, you have made me feel better. Let us go out and dine handsomely. I will take you to my favourite restaurant—it is in the Rue de Rivoli and—'

She was scarcely listening. Mrs Westover was found. She was in Paris, and Monsieur Reynaud was on her heels. He had found her and he was confident that he would find the pictures—and a bargain would be struck, and throughout not one word would be said about the real owner of the pictures. The real owner—the Professor, Professor Justin couldn't-care-less Hallam, was over there in

147

England eating boiled potatoes and allowing a bunch of crooks to cheat him.

Rage rose and almost choked her. Controlling herself as well as she could, she brought her mind back to Monsieur Reynaud.

'I'm sorry,' she said. 'I can't go out. My fiancé is in Paris and I'm expecting him.'

He said no more. She went downstairs with him and watched him get into the big car and be driven away. Then she walked slowly upstairs.

Before her, on the small table on which she had placed it, she saw the little package which Mrs Westover had left for her aunt. Without pausing to consider, she went over, picked it up and opened it. Inside was a small, white box; inside that, resting on cotton wool, was a small, gleaming object. She had never seen it before, but she recognised it instantly.

It was Diana Bannerman's sea-horse.

CHAPTER SIX

She did not know how long she stood there— but when at last she moved, it was with swiftness and purpose. She had only one idea: to get in touch with the Professor. He could no longer stand aside watching events with amused tolerance. His housekeeper could no longer be regarded as honest; she was handling stolen property.

She discarded the idea of using her aunt's telephone; she was discouraged from making even local calls. She put on a coat and ran downstairs; as she went, she heard the telephone in the flat ringing. She ignored it. She opened the street door, remembered that she had come down without a latchkey, ran upstairs and fetched one. The telephone was still ringing. She ran downstairs and out into the street; she would have to telephone from the café on the corner—not on the corner close by, but at the other end. As she hurried down the street, she saw a man about to enter the café; she raced him by a yard. Then she came out again; before telephoning, it was necessary to know the number. It was also necessary to have money. She hurried back to the flat, looked up the number of the farm, picked up her purse and went out again. Rain had begun to fall; she was without headscarf or umbrella. In a moment, drops that felt icy were trickling down her face and down the back of her neck. But her fear of undue delay in getting through was happily not realised; after standing, receiver to ear, listening to a confusion of sounds in French and English, hearing foreign or familiar exchanges named, she could distinguish at last the dialling sound that meant she was connected with the farm.

Al answered the telephone. It was a pity; any of the others could have been induced to summon Red, but Al's curiosity had first to be satisfied.

'*Who* ja say?'

'Mrs Abbey. Look—'

'No, she's gorn. She went away. Who's that wanting her?'

'Nobody wants her. This is Mrs Abbey speaking, Al. Will you please go and call Red? Quickly.'

'I thought you'd gorn away to Paris, or something.'

'I did. Will you please—'

'You don't mean you're *speaking* from there?'

'Yes. Will you please go and—'

'Mum! Grandie!' screamed Al. 'Come'n hark at this. It's Mrs Abbey. Roz! Come here. It's Mrs Abbey talking all the way from Paris.'

'Al, I want RED.'

'Red, she wants you. Red, she's talking from Paris. Mrs Abbey, it is. Oh Roz, let poor Mum have a look in, will you? Come on, Mum—can you hear her? Now your turn, Roz.'

'Roz, go *away*!' Lucille shouted. 'Send Red, quickly.'

She heard sounds of a fierce quarrel. The receiver was dropped, picked up and snatched away; there were loud arguments and, finally, tears. At last Red's voice came through.

'That you, Mrs Abbey?'

'Oh, thank *goodness*! Red, can you hear? Send ... those ... others ... *away*. Can you

150

hear me?'

'Sort of. Oh Dot, get *out* of it. Stop howling; how d'you expect me to hear anything? Mum, get 'em away, will you?—That's it. Go ahead, Mrs Abbey.'

'Red, I want to send the Professor a message.'

'Spout,' invited Red.

'Will you tell him that Mrs Westover is in Paris, and—'

'What—old Westie? What's she doing there?'

'That's for the Professor to worry about. Tell the Professor I've seen her.'

'She know anything about the pichers?'

'That's for the Professor to find out. Red, you'll tell him soon, won't you?'

'Leave it to me, Mrs Abbey. I'll see to it.'

'Thank you, Red. Goodbye.'

Exhausted, she crept out into the street, surprised to find no crowd assembled; she thought she must have roused the neighbourhood with her yells.

She walked slowly back to the house, heedless of the rain. From an upper window, Monsieur Boulanger, who had long delighted her by being the baker, leaned out and waved unsteadily; he was always a little exhilarated on Saturday nights.

'Oh, it's loff-ley to be joll-ee,' he sang; it was the only English he knew 'To be be be be be be be be be be joll-ee...' He leaned farther out,

151

and she feared for his safety. 'Misses Abb—ee.'

'Goodnight, Monsieur.'

A gentlemen, he told her, had called to see her. A gentleman undoubtedly English. Tall, handsome—the gentleman with whom she had gone out the evening before. He had come. He had rung the bell. He had looked up at the windows. He had rung the bell again, and again. He had gone away. Oh, it was loffley to be joll-ee ...

Lucille went upstairs to the flat, hung up her wet coat and went unashamedly to the medicinal bottle of cognac. Glass in hand, she mopped her damp face and neck; then, kicking off her shoes, she sat on the sofa, put her feet up and gave herself up to the inexplicable feeling of happiness that flowed through her. A confusion of names came and went in her brain: Malcolm, Monsieur Reynaud, Mrs Westover, Miss Clitheroe, Diana Bannerman—that was where the sea-horse came in. Malcolm ... He had come and gone. Good old Malcolm, to come and go. He hadn't enjoyed being folded up and fitted into the back of that car; naughty, naughty temper ...

Hazily, she heard the bell. Telephone? Door? Door. Malcolm had come, and gone ... and come again.

She went down as she was: stockinged feet, glass cradled in her hand. It was Diana Bannerman.

'Can I come in, or is it too late.'

152

'It is never too late,' Lucille said soberly.

'I wanted to talk to you. I . . . Anything the matter?'

'Nothing is the matter. Come in. Come up.'

'What's that you're drinking?' Diana enquired at the top. She sniffed the contents of the glass. 'Oh, that's it, is it? I suppose you've had a big row with Donne, and you're—'

'I went out and got wet. There has been no row. I haven't set eyes on the man you call Donne since he left the Three Bears.'

'Is this the stuff you're drinking? I'll join you.'

'It's my aunt's best brandy.'

'It was.'

'It's very strong. You shouldn't drink it; you're driving.'

'I'm not driving. I didn't come in a car. I had an argument with a silly fat man on a corner; when I say an argument, I mean that he abused me, while I told him I didn't parlez whatever language it was he was using.'

'What was he abusing you for?'

'He said I knocked him off his bicycle. He was lucky I did, because the car's in the garage now, having the bicycle scraped off. I was on my way to see you; I took a taxi the rest of the way. Have you eaten?'

'No.'

'That accounts for it. What made you think you could take that kind of drink on an empty stomach? Let's go out. No, don't let's. I hate cosy meals as a rule, but this time, one's indicated. Are you in a fit state to cook omelettes?'

'I wish you wouldn't keep hinting that I can't drink a little brandy without falling under the t … table.'

'If you've only had a little, you must have been in an excited state. Why? No, don't tell me yet. Food first.'

She carried a cushion into the kitchen, put it on a chair and sat down to watch Lucille preparing a meal. Lucille made mushroom omelettes, warmed some soup and carried the things to the dining-room. She opened a bottle of wine. They were about to sit down when the doorbell rang.

'Leave it to me,' Diana said firmly. 'This'll be that old English relic. I'll open the door, he'll see me and run for his life. I don't want to come between a man and his love, but if you're crazy enough to marry him, he'll have you for the rest of his life. He can spare you for tonight.'

She went downstairs with a determined air. Lucille waited. He would be angry, and she didn't think she was in a state of mind clear enough to cope with an angry man.

'It's a girl,' Diana called from below. 'She's howling; I'd better bring her up.'

Lucille went to the top of the stairs; she did not need to look; this could only be Miss Clitheroe.

'I had to c-come,' the visitor sobbed. 'It's

154

late, but I couldn't face walking into the dining-room at the hotel and sitting down all by myself. And Mr Donne won't talk to me. He dodges me.'

'This is Barbara Clitheroe, Diana.'

'Another candidate for a good, strong drink. Leave her to me,' said Diana.

When Lucille called them to the dining-room, they were firm friends. Barbara was still weeping, but intermittently.

'Why cry about china?' Diana asked. 'Or is it the man you're crying about?'

Barbara told them, convincingly, that she never wished to set eyes on him again.

'But it was a mean, low trick,' she said. 'My mother and I loved that china.'

'I haven't quite gathered why you couldn't go to the police,' Diana said. 'Or is it too sordid a tale?'

Barbara hesitated. But the little room, the candlelight, the gleaming table, the food and the wine were having their effect. Always disposed towards confidences, she now needed not only sympathy but advice.

'It was my father's,' she explained, 'but I suppose he felt that he'd left plenty to my mother and to me—so when he died, we found he'd parcelled out the china to distant relatives. My mother couldn't believe it at first—and then she said she'd never let it go. So she hid it. She put it away in a safe place and said it was all very well to leave pieces in his will, but he'd got rid of the china before he died, and there was none to dole out. She offered to give the equivalent in money, but only a few of them would take it; the others thought she was up to something.'

'How long did she keep it out of the way?'

'Not for long. After the big row there was over it, none of my father's family came near us. So there it was, but we never told anybody its real value. Even when I was engaged, even before my fiancé began to behave in what my mother said was a funny way, as if he didn't want to go through with it, we never said anything about the china's real value. But he must have known. And how could we call the police? If anything about valuable china got into the papers, look what would have happened.'

'Father's family forming up for a fight,' Diana said.

'Yes. And so when the Professor said to go to private detectives, I thought it was a good idea—but now I don't. I don't want to go chasing any more. I'm sick of it. I hope one day somebody'll catch up with him, that's all.'

'If I catch him, I'll have him jailed,' Diana promised. 'Why don't you look for a man to look after you? A different type, naturally. You're not poor; you can bypass the tramps and toilers and go after the titles. That was a good piece of ... you say it, Lucille.'

'Alliteration.'

'You see? she's clever—and even she gets herself stuck with a tweed jacket clutching a brace of pheasants. Donne, I'm talking about. He must give all these Frenchies the creeps, walking round looking like a resurr ... resurr ...'

'—resurrection.'

'—of an English milord. Why can't you two girls be like me? Forget the false starts and go ahead and ... Lucille, where are you going?'

Lucille was going into the drawing-room. She returned holding the small package which Mrs Westover had left.

'What's this? A present?' Diana asked, mystified.

Lucille handed her the package.

'Open it,' she said.

Diana opened it. She sat motionless, staring at it. There was a long silence; Lucille and Barbara waited. At last Diana looked up slowly.

'Where did you get this?' she asked.

'A woman brought it to the shop this evening. It was meant as a present for my aunt.'

'Your aunt isn't going to have this. This is mine. And I'd like to ask her some questions—the woman who brought it here, I mean. Where is she?'

'I don't know. I could get the address for you.'

Diana was pinning on the brooch.

'Got any more wine?' she asked. 'This is a

157

celebration.'

Lucille was sorry when at last her guests went. She felt no less hazy than when they had come; through the haziness, her happy, carefree mood persisted. She looked at the uncleared dining table, opened the door of the littered kitchen and shut it again; she had never before gone to bed leaving dishes unwashed, but tonight she did not care; some of Diana's take-it-as-it-comes philosophy seemed to have communicated itself to her.

She had a warm bath and went to bed. From the street floated up the Saturday night sounds now familiar to her: Madame Baltard saying goodnight to her Saturday gentleman; like Madame Camille, she had a string of respectable, ageing, innocuous admirers. Saturday was reserved for the most favoured.

Monsieur Boulanger was calling to his cats, Bijou and Zizi. She missed the giggling return of the Lachaise girls, and their father's exasperated summons from an upper window.

She dreamt of the children at the farm. She wanted to get to them, to give them a message; all the doors were locked and she was hammering ... hammering ...

She awoke. The hammering was on the door of the flat.

Her heart beating fast with the suddenness of her awakening, she went to a window and opened it. Down in the street, a form in a long mackintosh, small case in hand stepped backward in order to look up at her.

It was the Professor.

She was at first unable to move. She could only stand there stock-still, leaning out. The rain, still falling, wet her face.

'When you've finished acting the balcony scene,' came the Professor's annoyed voice, 'perhaps you'd very kindly let me in.'

She went to the door, walked back to the window and closed it automatically and in a daze went downstairs. The Professor stepped inside, took off his dripping mackintosh, shook it vigorously in the street and then closed the door.

'The first thing,' he said, turning her towards the stairs and urging her up them, 'is food. I hope you have some in the house. I'm sorry to disturb you and your aunt, but—'

She spoke for the first time.

'My aunt isn't here.'

'Good then—'

'If my aunt were here, then I wouldn't be,' she explained earnestly. 'The only reason I come to Paris is—'

'Yes, yes. We'll go into all that afterwards. Have you got any bread and cheese and beer?'

'I think so.'

He followed her into the kitchen and stood looking round him with an air of distaste. He looked into the dining-room.

'Been having a party, I see. I hope there's something left.'

'It wasn't a party. It was only Diana Bannerman first, and then Barbara Clitheroe came. Don't you remember Miss Clitheroe?'

'Clitheroe? The dreadful woman who came brandishing a piece of paper at me?'

'Yes. She—'

'Well, later. I'm hungry.'

'It was because of you that she came to Paris. She went to those private detectives, as you advised her to. She hasn't found the china yet, but Miss Bannerman has got her sea-horse back.'

He looked at her sharply.

'Party? Orgy,' he diagnosed. 'What's the matter with you? Is this the effect Paris has on you?' He opened the refrigerator and peered in. 'There's a bit of cold veal; that could do to begin with. Cheese; not much, but enough. Beer?'

'No. There's some wine.'

'So I see. One bottle of cognac, empty. One large bottle of white wine, empty. Two large bottles of red wine, drained. Ah, bread. Have you any with less crust and more crumb?'

'No. That's all you can get in Paris.'

'Then things have changed since last I was here. I used to get cottage loaves without any trouble at all. I don't care for this Indian-club type of loaf. Butter—is this all you've got?'

'I'm afraid so. The onions are here.'

'Did I ask for onions?'

'No, but you always do.'

160

'Ask for onions?'

'Eat onions. I'm sorry there isn't more food. Miss Bannerman suggested our going out for dinner, but she had left her car to have the bicycle scraped off it, and—'

'Perhaps,' said the Professor, studying her, 'I woke you up too suddenly. You sound a little confused.'

'I'm not at all confused. So would you be, if things had happened so fast. When she handed me that parcel, how could I guess that the sea-horse would be in it? But when Monsieur Reynaud went away, I opened it and there it was.'

There was a pause.

'Perhaps,' the Professor suggested at last, 'you'd better leave me to get myself some food. We can continue this discussion in the morning.'

'I was only trying to tell you what happened after Monsieur Reynaud left.'

'Perhaps you'd better begin by explaining when Monsieur Reynaud was here.'

'It was this evening—I think. I was just closing the shop when this woman came in; as I'd never set eyes on her in my life, how could I be expected to know who she was?'

'And who expected you to know who she was?'

'I've just told you: Monsieur Reynaud. He said he didn't want to call me a liar, but that's what I looked like. He was angry, and I'm not surprised; after chasing all round Canterbury, it must have been galling to find her out there, chatting to me. Or so he thought.'

After another glance at her. The Professor found a tray and proceeded to assemble his finds on it. He carried it into the drawing-room and put it down on a table and drew up a chair.

'At home,' he said, 'you always cleared up before going to bed.'

At home? Well, yes, she decided, perhaps he could call it that. Perhaps she thought of it like that. He looked at home now, his long nose pointed downwards, his hands busy buttering crusts of bread. Everything seemed to her entirely natural; even the reflection of herself, in a nightdress, seemed normal.

'There's milk,' she said. 'Would you like some?'

'That's the first sane remark you've uttered since I arrived. Yes, thank you; I should like some milk. Cold.'

She brought it to him.

'There must be something wrong,' she said. 'Look at the way—I've only just realised it— look at the way he purposely didn't give me Mrs Westover's address. I mean her niece's address. He—'

'Mrs Westover's niece is here?'

'Yes. She was an art student. She's going to be married and live in my aunt's apartment.'

'Here?' the Professor asked, startled.

'No. The other one. At least, it's almost

162

certainly her and not Mrs Westover. But the strangest thing of all was her having the sea-horse. It—'

'If you say sea-horse again,' the Professor said, drinking the last of the milk and carrying the tray back to the kitchen, 'I shall have to find you some kind of sedative. Where can I sleep?'

'Sleep?'

'It is'—he looked at his watch—'exactly five minutes to five. I have been travelling since Red brought me your—he said, urgent message. I have been in carts, trains, an aeroplane and a taxi. I should now like some sleep.'

'You can't sleep here. There isn't anywhere where—'

'I understand that your aunt is away. Doesn't she have a bed?'

'But you can't sleep in my aunt's bed. She doesn't know you. I mean—'

'Since she is not using it, I think I may be allowed to use it. That sofa is too small.'

'But—'

'If you're entertaining any odd ideas about the conventions, I guarantee not to mention your lapse to anybody. Where are the sheets kept?'

'There's a good hotel quite near. Malcolm Donne is there, and Miss Clitheroe.'

'Mr Donne is, I assume, your fiancé. Miss—'

'It isn't settled. It wasn't going too well, but when Miss Bannerman pushed him into the back of the car, he got angry. He left me at the

163

Three Bears and said I was to ring him up, but how could he expect me to, when so many important things suddenly came up?'

'He will no doubt take the matter up with you. Is there another pillow? Where Miss Clitheroe is, I would rather not be.'

'She's decided to go back to England in a few days. She isn't going to look for the china any more. But the sea-horse is different; Mrs—'

'This sea-horse is an ornament?'

'It's a brooch.'

'Thank you. As it seems certain to recur, we may as well identify it. I think you should go to bed.'

'Yes. But if Diana Bannerman hadn't come over here to visit her future relations-in-law, I'd never have known about the sea-horse, and I would have given it to my aunt.'

'You are now making contradictory speeches. Will you kindly make your aunt's bed, or shall I?'

She made it, listening to his splashes in the bathroom. He came out shamelessly in his shirt, climbed into the tapestry-hung four-poster and drew the sheets up to his chin.

'Grandmamma, grandmamma, what a big nose you've got,' he murmured sleepily. He closed his eyes and opened them again to look at Lucille.

'Your room,' he told her, 'is across the passage.'

'I'm going. But having come all the way

164

here, why can't you listen? I'm trying to put you into the picture. You don't known the full story. How can you just go to bed without finding out everything that's been going on? I've been trying to tell you what's happened; trying to...'

It was no use trying any more. He was asleep.

CHAPTER SEVEN

Somebody was moving in the kitchen when Lucille opened her eyes. So deeply had she slept that at first she imagined it to be her aunt; then recollection brought her fully awake.

She saw that it was seven o'clock. She washed, combed her hair, put on a dressing-gown and went to the kitchen. The Professor was seated at the table, drinking a large cup of hot, strong aromatic coffee.

'Good morning,' she said. 'I hope you slept well.'

'My feet stuck out at the end of the bed and got rather cold. You must have rather a head this morning, after your last night's orgy.'

'Did you make coffee for one, or coffee for two?'

'Coffee for one. I looked into your room; you were full fathoms five.'

'How can you sit here with all this mess

round you?' she asked. The room made her shudder. The dirty plates and dishes of the night before had been stacked, but not washed, a glimpse of the dining-room, so far from its usual polished self, made her put on an apron and go to work clearing up.

'You can't expect me to clear up after a party I didn't attend, can you?' the Professor asked.

'I never expect you to do anything—except for yourself.'

'You mean I should have made coffee for you, and left it to get cold?'

'Some men would have brought me in a tray with a teapot, milk and sugar, slices of lemon, toast, little curls of butter and a tiny pot of honey.'

'And a pale pink rose in a glass; don't forget that. I thought you'd rather be left to sleep it off. It was interesting, when I arrived, to see you with your usual cool head heated by wine.'

'For positively the last time, may I tell you that I had very little wine indeed?'

'You must have a weak head for drink. You sounded all but delirious.'

'I was tired, and I didn't expect you.'

'Why not? You telephoned—an expensive thing to do. Red said you sounded as though the matter was urgent—so I came. I'm here. You haven't, so far, made me understand why I'm here, but perhaps, later in the day, you'll feel equal to telling me. May I have my bath first, or does the water run out? If it does, I'll have my bath first.'

'There's plenty of hot water.'

Nevertheless, he used most of it; she had forgotten that most men filled a bath to the brim, sat in it and sent waves of water over the bathroom floor and bespattered the walls with soapsuds. She had to recall the Professor to clean the dark ring he left round the side—travel stains, he explained, as he worked to remove them.

'Why are there travel stains in the basin too?'

'I had to wash my socks. I only brought one spare pair.'

'I'll buy you two more spare pairs as soon as the shops open on Tuesday.'

While she was in her bath, she heard him go out; when she let him in some time later, he was laden with bread, butter and ham and eggs.

'Nice little food shops down the road,' he said. 'And nice people in charge. They all seem to think highly of you.'

She wondered whether they would think less highly of her after this, but she did not say so. She laid a place for the Professor in the dining-room, and served his breakfast.

'Aren't you eating?' he asked.

'No. All I want is coffee.'

'Perhaps you're wise. Do you feel ready to piece together all those disconnected fragments of information you gave out last night—or rather, this morning?'

'I can't piece them together. That's what I

sent for you for: to piece them together. Monsieur Reynaud left your house and went to find Mrs Westover in Canterbury. He found her. She said she hadn't taken the pictures. He didn't believe her, and he let her see that he didn't believe her. He went back to see again, only to find that she'd left. He found that her niece had been an art student here; he found out her address, but when he went there, he saw Mrs Westover getting into a taxi. He followed her here and saw me going out of the shop with her and concluded that I knew her. I didn't know her; she had come to the shop merely to give me a present for my aunt—the present I discovered later to be a—'

'—sea-horse.'

'—which had been stolen a few years ago from Miss Bannerman. Those are the facts. All through this matter of your mother's pictures, you've maintained that Mrs Westover hadn't taken them and wouldn't be able to make anything of them if she had. Do you still think so? Do you—after seeing Monsieur Reynaud's face when your mother's rooms were opened, after knowing the trouble he's been to to trace Mrs Westover—do you still think so?'

'I still think so.'

'She can be in possession of stolen jewellery, and still—in your opinion—be a blameless, harmless, honest woman?'

'If she knows it's stolen, why is she going round handing it out openly? I don't think she

168

has got my mother's pictures. If she'd wanted them, she could have had them, and welcome.'

'Your father thought those pictures worthless, and probably told you so, from the time you were a small boy. Hasn't it ever occurred to you that you're seeing them through his eyes, and not your own?'

'Why do you feel so passionately about this?'

'All I feel passionately about ... against ... is seeing a cheat getting away with something. Those pictures must, must, *must* have some value. Men like Paul Reynaud don't waste their time for nothing. He knows something about your pictures—your mother's pictures—that you don't know. It looks as though Mrs Westover knows it too.'

'Why should I begrudge Reynaud his profits? He's worked hard enough for them.'

'All I want you to do is to take steps to prevent yourself from being cheated, fleeced, done down. Being cheated isn't pleasant. It leaves you with a nasty taste. It strips something from you—something from inside you. I *know*.'

He said nothing for a time; his eyes were on her, studying her.

'So you want me to get hold of Mrs Westover,' he said at last. 'Is that it?'

'Yes. Today.'

'Don't I remember your saying something about not having her address?'

'I know a way of finding it out. She was

169

wearing one of Madame Baltard's hats.'

'Do we care what she was wearing? We want—'

'Madame Baltard will know where she lives.'

'Just because she bought a hat there?'

'You don't "just buy" one of Madame Baltard's hats. You have one of her hats made for you, just as you'd have a suit made for you. You go there and choose what you want. You go back for fittings. Naturally, you have to give your name and address. So we'll go to Madame Baltard and ask her.'

'Now?'

'No, not now. If you'll pack, I'll give you a lift to the hotel—I'm calling a taxi and I can drop you.'

'Where are you going?'

'To church.'

'Then I'll come with you.'

'How do you know where I'm going?'

'To church. You've just said so.'

'But how do you know which church?'

'Oh—denomination? What does it matter? The point is to get down on your knees, isn't it? What does it matter where? Are you going to pick up this fiancé of yours?'

'He isn't my fiancé. He's a Catholic. He'll go to Mass.'

'Aren't we Catholics? That's pity; I was going to suggest the Madeleine. Last time I went in, it was too dark to see anything; perhaps they've dusted the windows. I'm ready

170

if you are.'

They stopped at the hotel. She took the Professor inside and waited while he booked a room. Enquiring for Malcolm, she learned that he had left about an hour ago; he had left no message, but could be found at the Charlemagne. Miss Clitheroe had not yet come downstairs.

With the Professor, she went back to the taxi. They drove to church and he sat beside her following the service with an interest that looked suspiciously as though he were following it for the first time. He sang the hymns with revivalist fervour and a total disregard for pitch.

They had gone in leaving cloudy weather; they emerged into sunshine so brilliant as to have the quality of a blessing. The sky looked blue and benign; Paris was smiling.

They walked slowly—not homewards, not hurriedly. They strolled in the sunshine, pausing to watch children playing, stopping to see the swirl of cars round the Place de la Concorde. They made a half circle, crossed a street or two and found themselves at the church of La Madeleine. They went up the steps; the sound of music floated out. They went in and stood listening to the end of the Mass; at its conclusion, they went out and found themselves caught up in a crowd moving at a leisurely pace—all, it seemed, in one direction.

'I remember this,' the Professor said. 'The

Parisian parade. The Boulevard browse. If we go on drifting, we'll find ourselves at the Rue Montmartre—but you don't notice the distance; there's too much to see. Life. You can look at it without involvement. Your trouble is that you study your neighbour too closely; you study his requirements, you see that he gets his coffee before you get yours—Pff!' He cracked his fingers with such force that two small boys gazed up at him with wonder. 'You haven't enough detachment. You ... Look, you fellows, *votre mère* is showing signs of *colère*; I'd stick with the family if I were *vous*.'

'Is that all the French you posses?'

'My French is perfect—on paper. What was I saying?'

'That one needn't ever do anything for anybody else.'

'I meant to say that there are some forms of service which are, so to speak, small change. People—grown-up, fully-developed people are usually capable of seeing to their own needs.'

'Are you talking about service or chivalry?'

'On the level of chivalry, men may serve women—but is it really necessary to propel the modern woman tenderly across the street holding her elbow? Must a man hop like a flea from side to side to take the outside place every time they cross to another pavement? Does a man really have to struggle out of a well-sprung chair every time a woman comes in, goes out, comes in, out, in? Must he push a chair under her every time she sits down to soup? Must he take off his hat in pouring rain because a member of the opposite sex has bowed to him. Can't she enter a car without making him shut her door before scampering round to the driving seat? Must he do all those trivial, meaningless things?'

'Yes, he must. They're not meaningless; they're symbolic.'

'Still? When women have shed every outward sign of femininity? I might have seen some point in holding my hat twelve inches above my head while bowing to a ravishing creature with a delicate waist, a billowing bosom, spreading skirts and a confection of a hat—but today? Look at yourself: elegant, but tailored. Look at that woman over there.'

'Yum, yum.'

'You *like* it?'

'I could tear it off her.'

'You call her feminine?'

'Inside. And if you fail to accord her the usual signs of respect, she feels hurt.'

He turned to look at her.

'You got hurt?'

'No. I got inoculated the first time I saw you. It was plain that no chivalry stirred in you.'

They had been talking only intermittently; there had been long easy silences during which they had watched those who were passing them, those who approached. Sometimes they became separated; to prevent this, Lucille put a

173

hand on the Professor's arm and he drew it up until it rested in the crook of his elbow. The heat became oppressive; they discussed moving to the shady side of the street, but stayed where they were.

'Tired?' he asked at last.

'No, but I'm hungry.'

'Then let's eat. I haven't got any French money—only English.'

'How did you pay for your taxi this morning?'

'In English money. When it's English money or nothing, they take English money. You'll see in the restaurant.'

'I'm sorry—I shan't be able to lunch with you. Malcolm has no idea where I am.'

'Do you have to lay a trail, as in paperchasing?'

'We had a disagreement; it's time we made it up.'

'You were talking about chivalry. Shouldn't the man make the first move?'

'How can he, if he doesn't know where to find me? I'm going to his hotel—the Charlemagne.'

'Chivalry compels me to escort you. With luck, your fiancé will offer us both lunch. Thus I shall be able to save my English money.'

They came upon Malcolm in the splendidly-decorated entrance hall; Lucille had to admit that this was a more suitable setting for him than the homely little hotel he had left. He

174

came forward to meet her, but his greeting was cold.

'I've been trying to reach you,' he said. 'What happened to you last night?'

'I was only out for a little while. I—'

'Let's talk over lunch, shall we? Do you mind eating in the hotel? It's rather late to go out. I'm hungry.'

'She's hungry too,' the professor observed.

There was a tense pause. He had been at Lucille's elbow, but it had not occurred to Malcolm that they could be together. Something in his expression made Lucille turn and, for the first time since his arrival, make a detached study of the Professor's appearance.

It was hardly in keeping with these surroundings. His suit was creased, his tie crooked; his hair was untidy and too long. His trousers were too short. He was utterly unaware, or uncaring, of the figure he cut in the deeply-carpeted, plush-and-velvet hall—but Malcolm was only too conscious of the glances being turned in their direction. Attention of this kind, Lucille knew, was agony to him.

'This is Professor Hallam,' she said. 'I worked for him. Professor, Mr Donne.'

'Ah,' said the Professor.

''do,' muttered Malcolm. 'I wonder if you'd excuse us? I'd like to hurry Lucille in to lunch.'

The mood in which she had entered— friendly, conciliatory—vanished. Anger of a kind she rarely felt filled her. She said nothing;

175

she merely resisted the pressure of Malcolm's hand on her arm.

The Professor was preparing to leave.

'I'm glad you'll be paying the bill, and not me,' he told Malcolm. 'She didn't touch a thing for breakfast. I did my best to persuade her, but I think she had rather a headache after her night's little debauch. I could hardly sleep for the fumes.'

Malcolm stared at him speechlessly. The Professor raised a hand in farewell, walked a few steps and then returned.

'Oh—how about this hat shop?' he said to Lucille. 'Where shall we meet?'

'Will you come to the flat after lunch, please?'

'I'll be there. *Au revoir*, as they say here.'

Once more he retraced his steps.

'I'd like to buy one of those English newspapers,' he said. 'I can hardly offer them English pound notes.'

Lucille opened her purse and counted out some small change.

'Thank you. At the flat after lunch.'

This time, he did not return—but Malcolm had not moved.

'Is he mad?' he enquired. 'Is he off his head?'

'Would it have hurt you to offer him lunch?'

He was too astonished to note her white, set face.

'Offer him lunch? Offer … him …'

'If I'd dreamt you could be so … so rude, so

176

mean, so . . . I would have stayed and had lunch with him. I came here because I didn't like to think of you trying to get in touch with me and—'

'Your Paris friends seem to me to be a distinctly odd lot. Not to say a job lot. I'm not prepared to be seen in company with—'

'You ought to be proud to be seen with a man as distinguished as Professor Hallam.'

'He looked as though he'd come in looking for cigarette ends. I couldn't believe you were together. Didn't you see everybody staring? Do you realise that this place is full of English people who might know me? Do you realise who that man is, standing at the reception desk?'

'I don't care if he's two Cabinet Ministers. You—'

'We shall, if you please,' he said, taking a firm grip on her arm and propelling her towards the dining-room, 'continue this discussion elsewhere.'

They were placed at a corner table; next to them, seated alone, was an old, regal-looking lady to whom Malcolm bowed with something like deference. Then he seated himself opposite Lucille and made an attempt to conquer his ill-humour.

'Would you like something to drink first?' he asked.

'No, thank you. Didn't you hear the Professor say I drank too much last night?'

177

He put down the vast menu behind which he had retreated.

'You wouldn't care to explain that, I suppose? He used the word debauch.'

'It means to indulge in revelry. Your trouble is that you don't. Your trouble is that you imagine everybody's got their eyes fixed on you, wondering who you're with. Whom you're with. Your trouble is that you can only see the outside of people, not their insides.'

Waiters surrounded them, awaiting orders.

'Will you tell me what you'd like to eat?' Malcolm asked in an unnatural, *pas-devant-les-domestiques* voice.

She felt almost faint with hunger, humiliation, rage and disappointment. Last night's exhilaration, this morning's happiness, had been swept away by the cold, unsympathetic manner of the man sitting opposite. To have cut short the carefree hours in the Professor's company, to have come here with some sort of attempt to patch what was past repair, seemed to her almost pathetic in its uselessness. To have stayed, watching the Professor going away, alone and shabby, his newspaper under his arm...

'What will you have?' Malcolm repeated. 'I can recommend the pâté; they do an excellent one. After that perhaps you'd care for some—'

'I want cold chicken, potatoes in their skins, lots of butter, raw onions—and milk to drink,' she said.

It was said rather loudly. The colour leapt to Malcolm's face; his glance went from left to right, resting in near-panic on the regal old lady who was helping herself to *ragoût*.

'Will you kindly pull yourself together?' he hissed.

But Lucille was past caution—nor, she saw, was there any need for capitulation. Instinct told her that everybody within hearing was on her side. She remembered that Malcolm, for all his virtues, was only popular within his own circle; outside it, he was not liked. Waiters, lunchers—all, she knew now, were solidly behind her.

'Cold chicken,' she repeated firmly. 'And—'

'Is this a joke?' he demanded.

'It's the lunch the Professor and I always had. Almost always.'

'Did I understand him to say that you had breakfast together?'

'Quiet!' she warned. 'People can hear you. We couldn't have had breakfast together, because I didn't have any breakfast. That's why I'd like you to hurry up and order something.'

'You'll have pâté and lobster.'

'*You'll* have pâté and lobster. I'll have cold chicken—that's right; he's writing it down. And salad, please. One thing about a debauch is that it leaves you terribly empty. The Professor said I slept so heavily that he wouldn't wake me. He said that—'

179

What else the Professor said would never be known. Malcolm, with an abrupt movement, had pushed back his chair. The waiters gave way. Forty pairs of eyes watched him as he marched to the door and, without looking back, disappeared.

The regal lady was leaning sideways, looking at Lucille and blinking very fast to indicate that she wanted to speak to her.

'My dear, he wouldn't have suited you at all.'

'No,' agreed Lucille. 'I'm sorry if I disturbed your lunch.'

'You *made* my lunch! Won't you come and join me, and have your nice cold chicken here?'

Sympathetic arms moved Lucille's chair and carried her bag across to the other table. Smiles surrounded her; strangers at other tables bowed and raised their glasses in salute. It was, the Professor said, when she told him about it two hours later, heady stuff.

'Who paid for the lunch?' he enquired.

'The Comtesse. I've promised to go and see her before I leave Paris. I told her about my aunt's cosmetics and Madame Baltard's hats. Speaking of Madame Baltard, let's go.'

They rang the bell of Madame Baltard's flat; she led them up to a drawing-room plainer than Madame Camille's, but spotless, and smelling of floor-polish.

'I'm so sorry to disturb you on a Sunday,' Lucille said. 'We came to ask—it's rather

180

important—if you had the address of a lady who came into my aunt's shop yesterday, wearing one of your hats. She was English. She—'

'Grey-haired? Was it the lady who bought the model with the little ducks?'

'Yes. That's the one.'

'She is called Mrs Westover. Your aunt was kind enough to send her to me—it was a question of a wedding hat, but she also liked the little duck model, and so I made it for her.'

'She was a friend of my mother,' the Professor said. 'I would like to meet her again.'

'Please wait,' Madame Baltard said. 'The address will be in my order book; it is in the shop.'

She brought the address, written on a little white card. They thanked her and left.

'Far?' the Professor asked when they were outside.

'Not very far—but too far to walk,' Lucille told him. 'It's off the Avenue de Clairton; we'll have to get a taxi.'

The taxi stopped at the entrance to a long cul-de-sac. They got out and paid the driver; then they walked between tall, shabby houses, looking for the number. The houses had once been beautiful, but now they were spoilt by cheap and tasteless conversion. There were crude stairways leading to upper flats, balconies divided by wooden slats, front doors scarred by rows of electric bells.

181

They rang the bell of Number Seven, and waited. They had to wait for some time.

'Perhaps,' the Professor suggested, 'the bell's out of order.'

There was no way of telling; it would have rung—if it had rung—on the fourth floor. They stepped backwards and looked up—and as they did so, they saw a girl's head hurriedly withdrawn.

They rang again. After an interval, they heard a voice addressing them in French. The girl had reappeared.

'My name is Hallam—Professor Hallam,' the Professor called up to her. 'I came to see Mrs Westover.'

'I'm sorry. She's out.' The girl went away, and then came back with startling suddenness. 'Did you say Professor *Hallam*?'

'Yes.'

She hesitated.

'Wait, please,' she said at last.

They heard her footsteps as she came down the last flight of stairs. She opened the door; it was clear that she had not intended to ask them inside, but rain had begun to fall.

'You'd better come upstairs,' she said reluctantly.

They followed her inside.

'There's no lift; I'm afraid you'll have to walk up,' she said.

It seemed a long way. The flat at the top was so small that only the wide view to be seen from it saved the visitors from feeling that they were stepping into a box. There was a living-room; from it they glimpsed a tiny kitchen, a bedroom and a bathroom; all the rooms could have been fitted into the study at Hill House. The place was sparsely furnished, but there were flowers on a table near the window. On the table at the end of the room used for meals, Lucille saw a froth of white material and pieces of a paper dress pattern. She turned to the girl and looked for a moment at the slim figure, the dark eyes, the round, pretty little face. She could not have been more than nineteen.

'Wedding dress?'

For the first time, the girl smiled.

'Yes. I was going to have it made, but then I thought: Why not save the money? So I'm making it myself. Won't you sit down?'

'Will Mrs Westover be very long?' the Professor asked.

The girl faced him.

'Do you know who I am, Professor?' she asked.

'You are, I think, Mrs Westover's niece.'

'Yes. I'm Carol Westover. Will you tell me, please, why you're here? I mean,' she added, stopping him as he began to speak, 'will you tell me whether this is a ... a friendly visit?'

'What makes you think it isn't?' the Professor asked mildly.

'Because ... Hadn't we better sit down?'

They sat down; Carol Westover faced them,

183

and they saw she was close to tears.

'Could I ask you some questions, please?' she asked the Professor.

'Surely.'

'Are you here—here in Paris—purely on holiday?'

'No. I had a purpose in coming over.'

'Was that purpose connected with my aunt?'

'I would say not.'

'With your mother's pictures?'

'Yes.'

'Is it true that they were stolen?'

'I don't know. Who, I ask myself, would want them?'

'Do you believe that my aunt, Mrs Westover, could have taken them?'

'She *could* have taken them. Physically, there was no difficulty. They weren't large, they weren't heavy. She had trunks into which they would have fitted easily. They would, in fact, have fitted into a suitcase, and not a large suitcase. Yes, she could have taken them.'

'Do you think she did?'

'No. That is, I don't think she . . . purloined them, if that's what you mean. But there's always the chance that my mother and she had some sort of arrangement; my mother may have told her she could take them away with her if and when she left her post as housekeeper. Did my mother say something of the sort?'

'No. My aunt is quite certain that your

184

mother wouldn't in the least have objected to her taking the pictures, but as they weren't mentioned in your mother's will, she felt she had no right to them. When she left your house, the pictures were hanging on the walls. Please believe that.'

'It isn't difficult to believe. I have stated, since the beginning of this little misunderstanding that your aunt was not the type of person to do anything dishonest.'

'Thank you.' Two tears rolled down Carol's face. 'She'll be glad to know that.'

'Why can't I assure her of the fact myself?'

'Because she ... Because you can't see her today.'

'Tomorrow?'

'I hope so. You see, Professor, she's ... well, I advised her to move out of this flat until my fiancé came back. He's in England; he'll be back tonight and you can see him tomorrow and talk to him.'

'Why not to Mrs Westover?'

'To her, too—certainly. But she's upset. Someone has accused her of stealing the pictures.'

'Someone here?'

'In Canterbury—and now here, in Paris. She came over here to stay with me until my wedding. She was upset when she came, but when she told me what was worrying her— frightening her—I realised that this isn't just a simple case of the pictures your mother

painted. It's . . . there's more than that. And my
aunt and I are mixed up in it, and until my
fiancé gets back, I can't put you in touch with
my aunt. Other people are trying to get in
touch with her, too. She won't tell me who they
are, but she's frightened. I would be too, a
little, only I know we haven't done anything
wrong. I only wish I'd never seen the picture in
the first place.'

The tears were flowing fast. It was necessary
to wait until they were dried. Lucille left her
chair and went to sit beside the small, sobbing
figure.

'What's the matter?' she asked gently.
'There's nothing to worry about. Your fiancé
will come back, we'll all meet, the thing will be
cleared up—that's all.'

'No, it's not all.' Carol raised a tear-stained
face. 'You don't know about the other picture.'

'What other picture?'

The girl made a strong effort at control.
When she spoke, her voice was steadier.

'Perhaps I'd better tell you from the
beginning,' she said. 'Did you know that I was
an art student?'

The Professor nodded.

'Well, as an art student, I knew that the little
pictures your mother gave my aunt, and which
my aunt brought with her on her visits to the
flat we shared in Canterbury, were not very
good.'

'They were terrible,' said the Professor.

186

'Please go on.'

'But when my aunt left your house—when you told her you wouldn't be keeping her on, and said she was free to go—she didn't go to Canterbury; I persuaded her to come over and have a little holiday with me first. So she came, and she brought me, as her usual little present, a picture. It was one of those your mother had given her, one of those your mother gave her from time to time. I looked at it, and I realised it wasn't painted by your mother. It was...' She paused and looked from the Professor to Lucille. 'Have you ever heard of Anton Horst?'

The Professor had not. Lucille, after a moment, was able to say that she had seen his name in a newspaper, but in what connection, she was unable to remember.

'He's an artist,' Carol told them. 'It isn't surprising that you've never heard of him. Until a few months ago, nobody had ever heard of him. Since then, he's become art news. I don't like his work, but it's making money—a great deal of money. The picture my aunt brought over from England was by Anton Horst.'

There was a pause.

'Ah,' said the Professor at last. He gave a sigh of relief. 'So far,' he confessed, 'I have been very bored by all this reiteration—ever since we discovered the loss of the pictures, I have been unable to make any kind of sense out of the affair. But you have made me feel that it

187

might, after all, have some interest. Please go on.'

'I told my aunt it wasn't by Mrs Hallam—she said of course it was; anybody could see it was. It even had Mrs Hallam's—Amy Hallam's—initials. But I was sure it was a Horst. And to prove it, I ... we ... had it valued. It was a Horst. It wasn't worth as much as the later Horsts, but it was worth about four hundred pounds. We decided that we would accept the offer—but before going farther, we thought you ought to be told about it. So my aunt went back to England. She intended going to Hill House and telling you just what I've told you now—but before she could pay a visit to you, she was ... she was approached by somebody and accused of having stolen the pictures. You can see now what a terrible shock it was for her. She came straight back here, and she's here now, but she and I are waiting for my fiancé to ... to ...'

'To stand behind you?'

'In a way. We know we haven't done anything wrong; all the same, my aunt had a picture which she said was valueless and which in fact was worth what we think is a lot of money. Horsts are selling for four figures; soon they say they'll fetch five. Can you imagine how we feel?'

'You should feel happy. Four hundred pounds will buy a great deal of champagne for your wedding,' pointed out the Professor.

It was not possible to communicate his cheerful outlook to Carol; her hands were shielding her face and she was crying bitterly. Nothing—not even Lucille's offer to make her some tea—could check the flow.

'I ought to b-be making t-tea for you,' she sobbed. 'I'm so s-sorry ... but it's been so awful, with my aunt standing at the window looking to see who was coming, and both of us trying to pretend there was nothing wrong, and talking about the wedding, and dresses and hats, and the flat my fiancé rented for us, with the basement for his things, and deciding how much of this furniture to keep, and how much to buy...'

'Tomorrow,' the Professor promised, 'will see the end of it. Dry your tears.'

She did her best. She came with them to the door; they would not allow her to accompany them downstairs.

'We'll let ourselves out,' the Professor said. 'Please remember me to your aunt.'

'I will. I'm sorry our first meeting was so damp. I'm sorry I ... took it out on you, but I feel better.'

'I'm glad.' The Professor nodded towards the wedding dress. 'We interrupted you.'

'Is your fiancé French?' Lucille asked.

The girl's face lit up.

'Oh goodness, no! He's English—but we didn't meet until I came over here. One way and another'—a charming colour came to her

189

cheeks—'it's been a terrible rush.'

'Your aunt had a very pretty brooch which she—'

'Oh—the sea-horse? It's pretty, isn't it? My fiancé got it in a little shop in the Bastille district. He—look, won't you stay and let me make you some tea? Or is it too late for tea?'

'We can't stay, thank you,' Lucille said. 'Goodbye—and good luck.'

'Thank you.'

Out in the street, the Professor seemed thoughtful. It was Lucille who had to stop a passing taxi and direct the driver to the Rue des Dames. But he was not so deeply immersed in his musing as to be unaware that Lucille had suddenly twisted herself round and was staring after a car that had passed them.

'Yes, I thought so too,' he said.

She turned; their eyes met.

'Mrs Westover and—'

'Quite right. Our friend Monsieur Reynaud. Was she hiding from him, or from us?'

'Well, she's with him. Now he can ask her all the questions he wants to,' Lucille said.

'There's only one question he needs to ask her,' the Professor said slowly. 'I wish very much that I could put it to her myself.'

'Why?'

'Because when we know the answer,' the Professor said, 'we know everything.'

CHAPTER EIGHT

They arrived at Madame Camille's to find a car outside the door. In it, slumped sleepily in the driving seat, was Diana Bannerman.

'So you finally got back,' she said to Lucille. 'I nearly called the gendarmes. I thought last night must have knocked you right out.'

'This is Professor Hallam, Diana.'

'And you,' the Professor said, 'are the other half of the debauch. Are you also the sea-horse which was found in a shop in the Bastille district?'

'You've been investigating?' Diana asked. 'If so, stop. François—he's my fiancé—said he positively doesn't want any probing into the past. He says what's gone, went. Can't we go upstairs? I came to take Lucille out to lunch,' she explained, as they went. 'No sign. I came back. Still no sign. I went ring-ring and then I went bang-bang; no reply from Lucille but a lot of kind attention from the neighbours, notably a sweet little man with two dogs. Lucille, what have you done with milor'?'

'He left me,' said Lucille.

'You mean for good?'

'I think so.'

'You're not going after him, are you?'

'No.'

'Thank heaven you've seen him in his true

191

blight. Got a drink? I need one—and I need help.'

The Professor gave her the drink; it was from Lucille, it seemed, that help was to come.

'If the Professor would go away, I could howl.'

'There's something about me,' the Professor said musingly, 'that makes women cry. I've only lately discovered the fact.'

Diana was taking him in for the first time.

'It's the mother in them,' she said. 'Look at you: your clothes all anyhow, and one sock coming down. When did you appear? Nobody said anything about visiting professors.'

'Lucille sent for me. I travelled through the night; through most of the night. The last part of it I spent in Madame Camille's bed.'

'Without undressing, I can see that,' Diana said frankly. 'Did you meet that fellow Lucille nearly got entangled with?'

'Mr Donne? I exchanged courtesies with him.'

'Wasn't that enough to prove to you that he wouldn't have done as a husband for her?'

'If it had been, I wouldn't have presumed to tell her so.'

'Fat lot of help you are to your friends,' she said bitterly. 'You'd look on, you'd stand aside and watch them getting married to the wrong man. Like me at this moment. Lucille, I'm in trouble. I love François—you know I love him. But the more I see of his ghastly relations, the more I feel I'm not cut out to be a châtelaine.'

'If he has a château,' the Professor said, 'I should advise you to stifle your doubts.'

'Well, I can't. If he'd come and live in London, I'd marry him tomorrow—but he won't. He's rooted here in Paris, and he's surrounded by these awful kiths and kins. One: mother; a widow, and tight-fisted. Two: his pair of silly sisters. Three, no four: uncle, who's unfortunately the senior partner in the business. Five: another uncle. I've run out of fingers, but you couldn't count them all. They go on and on.'

'And when you get married, won't you be able to keep them out?' enquired the Professor.

'You've missed the point: François doesn't *want* to keep them out. He *loves* them. He wants *me* to love them. He's a great believer in love. He thinks that love will carry me through a French language course, turn me into a typical Parisienne, enable me to charm his mother and sisters and disarm the rest of the tribe.'

'Do they like you?'

'They can't bear me.'

'Then surely, once you're married, there will be no problem?'

There was a pause while Diana took this in.

'What you mean is that they'll keep away?'

'I think it very likely. Until you're married, they have—so to speak—to put a good face on it. As to becoming a typical Parisienne, I

193

imagine your fiancé is marrying you because he likes you as you are. Does he speak English?'

'Beautiful English.'

'Then let him use it.'

'But everyone knows that relations can wreck a marriage.'

'Nonsense.'

'So I have to live in Paris and never see London again?'

'A great many people would envy you. And is the distance between the two cities so great that—'

'Popping over isn't the same as being there. Speaking of popping over, why did Lucille send for you?'

'It's a long and complicated story.'

'Take your time. I told François I was going to use his car and take Lucille out to dinner. I don't think he heard, but I've got the car. Perhaps Lucille won't come when she hears that Miss Clitheroe's coming too.'

'Where did you meet her?' Lucille asked.

'She came twice while I was waiting for you—she walked round from that hotel. She's going away tomorrow, so I didn't see how I could avoid letting her come here tonight. And once here, just watch her settling down. Forlorn little thing, isn't she? All that money, and mother hiding the china and the fellow going off with it in the end.' She broke off and stared at the Professor. 'Why, you must be the one who advised her to go to those detectives!'

'She was crying. I had to say something.'

'Here she is,' Lucille said, as the doorbell rang.

The Professor went downstairs and returned with a woman who looked very far from the forlorn creature Diana had dubbed her. She was in a smart woollen suit and her hair was brushed off her face, giving her a schoolgirl look. She was, she said, leaving the next day.

'Well, now you're here, we can think about dinner,' said Diana. 'Any suggestions, Professor?'

The Professor did not hear. He was standing gazing out into the darkening street.

'Hey—Professor!' Diana called. 'We need you.'

He turned slowly, but there was no recognition in his eyes. His brow was furrowed; with his hands deep in his pockets, he was pursuing a line of thought to which they had no clue.

'It all hangs,' he muttered to himself, 'on the time angle.'

'What's the matter with him?' Diana demanded. 'Wave a hand in front of his eyes and see if he comes round.'

'I don't understand it.' The Professor was gazing at Lucille, addressing her as though nobody else were present. 'And of course, that was an obvious lie; you must have known that.'

'Who was lying?' Diana asked in bewilderment.

195

The Professor, oblivious to anything but his train of thought, continued to mutter to himself.

'It all comes down, as I said,' he decided, 'to time. And I think there was time; not much, but enough. If I could work out just how much, I could get somewhere.'

'Well, some other time,' Diana suggested. 'We've got to eat, Professor.'

'We've got to go back,' intoned the Professor, 'to the beginning. I assumed that the beginning was when my mother died—but I was wrong. The beginning was before that.'

'Look, could you take this up with Lucille some other night?' Diana asked him. 'We can't sit here waiting for you to work out whatever it is from the beginning. Let's go and eat. If you object to paying for all three of us—'

'He can't,' said Lucille. 'He's only got English money.'

'That's a new one,' commented Diana. 'Well, dinner's on me.'

'No. Dutch,' said Barbara.

'I should have got on to the art student angle earlier,' the Professor said. 'If I hadn't been so sure, from the start, that I could rule out dishonesty—'

'Couldn't we leave him here to rule it out?' Diana asked. 'He's gone into a trance.'

'He ought to eat,' said Barbara. 'Perhaps when he gets outside, he'll wake up. Let's take him along.'

'Look at his clothes,' Diana complained. 'How can we go anywhere decent with a man who looks like that?'

'Give me your coat,' Lucille ordered the unheeding Professor. 'I'll press it.'

They removed his coat and also, giving him a sheet in which to drape himself, his trousers. Barbara, working busily with a steam iron, hummed happily.

'Don't tell me you're enjoying it,' Diana said in surprise.

'But I am. I love anything to do with housework. Cooking, washing, ironing—I could keep at it all day long. That's why I want a house of my own—and a husband.'

'You can iron a man's clothes without marrying him. You're doing it now, in fact.'

'I want something permanent. I want a nice house with a man in it.'

'That's not hard to find, is it?'

'Yes, it is. Look at the way I found a man and he turned out to be a thief and...'

'Now I've started you off crying. You picked a dud, that's all. So did I. You don't see me crying, do you? If your eyes are full of tears, how can you see the next man looming up? If I'd been crying and moaning, the way you do, d'you suppose François would have fallen in love with me? All you've got to do is go back to England and get away from your mother and set up on your own; you'll soon get fixed up. Especially if you wear dresses like the one

197

you've got on, and do your hair like that. Give me those things and let's get the Professor dressed.'

'You can see,' the Professor was telling Lucille, 'that the niece couldn't have been connected with anything shady. At the same time, we have to remember that everything turns on her.'

'Brush his hair, somebody,' said Diana. 'And take those things out of his pockets— they're bulging. I don't think he needs dinner; I think he needs a week in a nice, quiet Home. That's better; now he looks fit to be seen with three beautiful women. When he comes round, he's going to get a fright—if he comes round. He'll think he's somebody else.'

'Will we all fit into the car?' Barbara asked.

They managed it by stuffing the Professor and Barbara into the back. He leaned forward and continued to address Lucille.

'The time factor's important,' he said, 'because until that Horst fellow began to get fashionable, nobody had any interest whatsoever in the pictures. And so we come to the beginning again: my mother's visit to Reynaud's studio.'

'Look, Diana,' Barbara begged in an agonised tone, 'couldn't you go a bit slower? You keep going into the middle of the road.'

'It's this steering wheel—it's got ideas of its own. Relax; there's six yards of engine protecting you. Shall we go to that Three Bears place again, Lucille?'

'If you like.'

'Reynaud's story,' intoned the Professor, 'was that my mother offered him her pictures. Lie number one. My mother was on her way back to England. My mother was in the habit of taking up promising artists. My mother—'

'There's a song that goes like that,' Diana said. 'She came from Oireland, or somewhere.'

'If we trace the rise of Horst,' the Professor said, 'we shall undoubtedly find that, for once in his career of unparalleled success, our friend Reynaud missed the bus. I don't think we can blame him; my mother's last, and worst, pictures were painted under the Anton Horst influence. I dare say they looked as unpromising to Reynaud as they did to me. And he must have got a little tired of elderly English ladies who offered him pictures—their own, or those painted by their protégés.'

'Do you know what he's talking about?' Diana asked Lucille as they entered the restaurant.

'Yes, I know. Let him work it out.'

'*Let* him? Who's got a hope of stopping him? No, not that table,' she said in a loud, firm voice to the waiter. 'I want that one over there.'

'Madame, you can see—it has a Reserved sign.'

'I know. It moves,' Diana told him.

She removed it and handed it to him, together with a note. She arranged her guests, took the menu with a sigh of satisfaction, and read out her suggestions.

'And so,' the Professor said, 'Reynaud, looking round and seeing Anton Horst's work soaring to the top of the popularity poll, goes in search of his pictures. But he cannot remember—for he was not especially interested—exactly which pictures he was offered. Discovering talent excited my mother very much. When excited, she was apt to become incoherent. I think Monsieur Reynaud had a hard time reconstructing her visit. But he finds her address, and he sets off in the hope of making a scoop.'

'Can people eat when they're like this?' Barbara asked. 'Doesn't the food sort of ball up in the stomach and make them ill?'

'They're a natural hazard for these professors, balls in the stomach,' Diana told her. 'These big brains often have these fits. Their wives have to tie labels on them so that people can lead them home. Lucille, why don't you have some of this delicious sauce? It's ... look, Barbara: she's getting glazed eyes too. She's forgotten all about food.'

'But while Monsieur Reynaud is hanging round waiting for the rooms to be opened, things are happening elsewhere,' went on the Professor. 'Mrs Westover has produced one of Horst's works.'

'You're going to get married soon, aren't you?' Barbara asked.

Diana nodded.

'Yes, I suppose life in Paris will have its compensations. This food, for example. And clothes. Did you know that Lucille got rid of that fellow she was nearly tied up with?'

'What happened?'

'I don't know any details. I'll ask her when she comes round. Do you suppose the Professor knows he's eating, or is he just shoving it in mechanically?'

'She said,' proceeded the Professor, 'that it was one of my mother's pictures. Her niece said it wasn't. They took it to be valued. If we knew where they took it, we should—I'm absolutely certain—know everything.'

'What does it matter where they took it? Any dealer, by that time, would have known a work by Anton Horst. Any dealer—'

'But suppose for a moment that it wasn't "any" dealer. And glance once more at the time factor. Cast your mind back to that piece of paper which Miss Clitheroe brought to Hill House.'

'He's dragging me into it,' Barbara moaned. 'Did you hear?'

'Oh, stop *crying*,' Diana said in exasperation. 'Haven't we got enough trouble? If he doesn't stop, he's going to give me a fit of the creeps.'

'You mean—now we come to a thief?' Lucille asked the Professor.

'Yes. There you have a third lead. You have

201

Monsieur Reynaud in London. You have Mrs Westover and her niece here.'

'But Mrs Westover went back to Canterbury.'

'Only for a short time. Only just long enough to meet Monsieur Reynaud and be frightened into returning to Paris. You may be quite sure he checked how long she was there. And if he's as astute as you've always claimed him to be, he didn't come back to Paris to accuse Mrs Westover. All he would want, and all I want now, would be to ask her just one question.'

'The dealer?'

'Yes. Nobody had the slightest interest in my mother's pictures—or shall we now say the pictures my mother had in her possession? Nobody—except, on the one hand, Reynaud, and—once Mrs Westover and her niece went to him—the Paris dealer. He would ask—wouldn't he?—where they got the Anton Horst. He would ask—surely?—whether they knew of any more. He would, undoubtedly, learn that there were pictures at Hill House.'

'But ... but why steal the china? Why not go straight for the pictures?'

'It's very easy, once you've seized a thread and followed it. Once you've made up your mind not to be side-tracked. Once you can build up the thing. Once you can rule out extraneous facts. You can see it ... nearly all. All that doesn't tie up is ...'

He stopped abruptly. Then, with a sudden

movement, he was on his feet, pushing aside his plate, overturning his chair, looking round wildly to locate the exit.

'Quick!' he shouted to Lucille. 'Quick—come on.'

'He's gone over the edge,' Barbara sobbed. 'We shouldn't have brought him.'

'Quick!' The Professor leaned over and seized Diana by the arm. 'Your car! Hurry!'

His wild gaze, his loud, decisive orders brought her to her feet.

'Humour him,' she muttered to Barbara. 'Don't cross him, whatever you do.'

She groped hurriedly in her bag, threw some notes on to the table and was urged by the Professor to the nearest door.

'Not that one, Professor,' she said in soothing tones. 'That's the powder room. If you're trying to get out, it's this way.'

He did not relax his grip on her arm; with his other hand he grasped Lucille. Behind them, tears of fright, mortification and unassuaged hunger pouring down her face, came Barbara.

There was difficulty getting into the car; the Professor could not at first be persuaded to let them enter singly. At last they were in; he was behind, leaning forward and digging Diana urgently on the shoulder.

'Leave off, you!' she shouted at last, in desperation. 'What do you think I am—a camel? If you prod me again, you'll get out and walk. Where in hell,' she asked Lucille, 'does he want to go? You'd better ask him.'

'Where are we going?' Lucille asked him.

'*Where?*' he repeated incredulously. 'You mean you don't know? Haven't I made it clear? We're going to your aunt's flat. Where else?'

'My aunt's flat?' she repeated in a dazed voice. 'My aunt's flat?'

'Haven't you seen *yet?*' the Professor shouted. 'It's as clear as daylight. If I'd given my mind to it before, I would have seen that the solution was not there, but here. Here, in Paris. And, since he's seen Mrs Westover, that's what Reynaud knows by now. One question only: *which* gallery did she and her niece go to with their Anton Horst picture? Which? So *now* do you see?'

'No.'

'Can't you work the thing out when the solution is placed in your grasp? Anton Horst's pictures become the rage. Reynaud goes off on his quest. He finds the pictures he's after—but he's too late. Why? Because in the meantime, two women, two straightforward, honest women have taken their picture to his gallery ... and walked into the lion's mouth. From then on, we had to follow not Reynaud, but the assistant Reynaud left in charge of his gallery. It *has* to be his gallery. At what other gallery would there have been this need to offer ... didn't you hear what that girl said? She was offered the paltry sum of four hundred pounds—not francs, mark you; pounds—for what she was told was an early Horst. Early? My mother met him in the spring—the spring of this year. The work in her possession could have been nothing but later Horsts—the latest Horsts. And late or early, the picture, having been valued, should have been offered for sale openly. Why would this assistant have made his own deal, unless he had his own plans? And why was it that some china was stolen? To obtain funds. To lay hands on some money with which to pay for Horst pictures. No; not Horst pictures. Only one Horst picture. He needed four hundred pounds. He would have to pay for one picture; he made different arrangements to lay his hands on the rest. And so we come back to Paris—always back to Paris. Horst is the rage, not as yet in England, but here in Paris. And so the pictures have to be here. The pictures are here. Hurry!' he urged, prodding Diana once more. 'Hurry!'

She stopped with a jerk outside Madame Camille's shop.

'No, no, no!' shouted the Professor. 'On! On to the corner!'

She stopped a few yards farther on. Behind them was the quiet, cobbled street. In front was the brilliantly-lit avenue.

'Round the corner!' directed the Professor.

Diana drove round and stopped at the front entrance. Ahead, parked against the pavement, was a large car: Monsieur Reynaud's.

205

The Professor fell out of the car.

'Here?' Lucille asked. 'But I haven't got the keys. The keys were given to the tenant. I—'

She stopped. The iron grille was being slowly drawn back. Monsieur Reynaud stepped down on to the pavement. He and the Professor stood looking at one another.

'We travelled by different roads,' the Frenchman said, 'but we have arrived together. He is inside. Shall we go in?'

He had spoken in a low voice. Motioning to the others for silence, he led them into the dark, spacious, empty showroom. The avenue lights showed them the door at the other end. They passed silently beyond it and found themselves in a smaller room.

There was no sound. The Professor and Monsieur Reynaud edged forward. Diana slipped her shoes off and held them in her hand. A low, nervous sob came from Barbara Clitheroe and was instantly stifled.

Cautiously, the Professor opened a door. One by one, they filed out on to a narrow wooden balcony.

Lucille was between the Professor and Monsieur Reynaud. There was very little light; the avenue was by now a mere glimmer in the rear. It was enough, however, to show them that they were standing on a narrow platform which ran round the wall above a central well. A wooden stairway led down to a large, double door—the entrance to the basement storeroom. Bending down to insert a large key into the keyhole, working by the light of a torch, they saw the figure of a man.

For about five seconds, nobody moved. Then something that had been born in Lucille's mind, that had grown there since her visit to Carol Westover's flat, that had been vague and formless, suddenly became a clear, horrible certainty. She stared down at the man's bent back—and then, before she or any of the others realised what she meant to do, she had raised her heavy bag and flung it downward and with deadly accuracy, straight on to the figure below.

The brass end caught the man squarely on the back of the head. He sagged; he fell sideways and for an instant lay bent—then he fell back and became motionless, his face upturned to the watchers on the platform above. And in the silence that followed, a choked cry was heard from Barbara Clitheroe.

'James!' she sobbed.

'*James!*' came in stupefied accents from Diana. 'James Tandy!'

Lucille made no sound. Staring down at the all-too-familiar countenance, she trembled, sick with rage and pity. But she was not thinking of herself. Her mind was on a little room, gay with flowers, and on a white froth of wedding dress.

... he'll be back tonight...

The Professor and Monsieur Reynaud were

looking at her.

'So you were his wife?' Monsieur Reynaud said slowly.

She nodded, too sick to speak.

'He was my assistant. He knew, of course, that I should find out everything—but if he had the pictures, what did it matter? He got the pictures. After stealing them from the Professor's house, I do not know where he kept them—but they are here now. He has just locked them up.'

'A flat for himself and his bride; a basement for the pictures,' the Professor said thoughtfully.

'He is the first man,' Monsieur Reynaud said solemnly, 'who ever came so near to cheating me. He is a clever man.'

'I don't think I'd call him a man; geiger-counter would be nearer the mark,' Diana said bitterly. 'He just turns naturally towards treasure.'

'We'll have to get him away,' the Professor said. 'He ought to be sent—'

'Not to that flat,' came sharply from Lucille. 'Not to ... not to that girl.'

'I will take him to my house,' said Monsieur Reynaud. 'When he feels better, we must have a little talk together. Professor, will you help me?'

The two men carried up the limp form. Out in the street, they felt it more prudent to drape the arms round their shoulders, and present an appearance of two friends assisting a third to his car. They placed him in front; Monsieur drove away with the unconscious man's head resting affectionately on his shoulder.

'Your handbag is still down there; I'll get it,' the Professor told Lucille. He brought it, and stood looking at the three women.

'If you're wondering how we feel,' Diana said hardily, 'we feel all right. A knock on the head isn't much retribution, but he's still got that Frenchman to deal with. That makes me feel better. What are you crying for now?' she asked Barbara.

'R-relief.' She fumbled in her bag for a handkerchief. 'I always hoped something would catch up with him.'

Diana was looking at Lucille.

'You're thinking of that girl, aren't you? His fiancée.'

'Yes, I am.'

'Well, don't. We lived through it. We survived. I daresay she will, too. D'you mind if we go up to the flat? I could do with some coffee—with something in it.'

They went up to the flat. They imagined the Professor to be following them, but he was nowhere to be seen.

'He's left us,' Diana said bitterly, 'to talk over old times.'

CHAPTER NINE

There was very little talk of old times. Diana, drinking scalding black coffee, summed up her feelings.

'Personally, I've no regrets,' she said. 'I think I got off cheaply. He was a good actor; I thought he loved me—but the thing began to work loose when he found my money was out of his reach. The jewels must have been some compensation. And the china,' she added, to Barbara. 'All I'd like to do is walk in and tell his fiancée a few things.'

'No,' said Lucille.

'Why not? She's got to find out, and who can tell her more about him than we can? Or you can; after all, you're the only one he got as far as marrying. There's one thing: I don't feel as sore as I did. After all, we were up against a professional; what chance did we have of seeing through him? What's this last fiancé of his like, Lucille?'

'Like I was at her age. Trusting, eager, happy and full of hope.' Her voice shook, and then steadied. 'There was something about that flat, when the Professor and I went in, that took me back to the time I was making my wedding dress. There was something about her that reminded me of myself. I couldn't have worked out any connection; assistants, fiancés,

210

pictures, china, galleries—the whole thing was confusion, but in that flat . . .'

'Would you like us to get out?' Diana asked.

'Yes, please. I'm sorry . . .'

'You're not going to sit and cry over that dirty crook, are you?'

'No.'

'Well, don't worry about the girl, either. What makes you think that she hasn't got our resilience?'

Lucille made no reply. They left her; left alone, she gave way to the helpless pity she felt for Carol Westover. What she had seen in her, she knew now, was her young self. She had seen a young girl standing, shy and eager, on the brink of marriage. A young girl without suspicion. A young girl scarcely able to believe in her own happiness, breathless from the speed with which events had moved. *It's been a terrible rush* . . . Yes, he would have to hurry. If one knew him, one did not need to be told details. Once she entered the Reynaud gallery with the Horst picture, a girl unaware of the fortune she was holding in her hands . . . It must have been easy. And to do him justice, he would, in his way, love her. He was a man of taste. He was a man capable of judging value— hers as well as her pictures. He was a cheat, but there were worse things than cheating. Marriage with him had been a time of happiness; the humiliation had outlived the happiness, but it was the kind of humiliation
211

that left no permanent scars. He could make a woman happy—until she found him out.

Through her absorption, she heard the sound of the bell. She opened the window and looked out.

'Too late for coffee?' the Professor called up to her.

She let him in and made some. The Professor helped himself to two large slices of bread, toasted them and spread butter on them.

'Your hotel,' she pointed out, 'would have provided food.'

'I saw those two women leave. I came back because I knew you had the Westover girl on your mind. I didn't go to the hotel; I went back to that basement to see if all the pictures were there.'

'And were they?'

'They were. But hanging about down there made me cold; this coffee's good. How much did the sight of that fellow upset you?'

'It didn't. Not in the way you mean.'

'Well, stop worrying about his fiancée. She isn't going to be disillusioned yet.'

'How long do you think he'll stay around now that he knows he hasn't got the pictures?' she demanded. 'I know they weren't hers, but he knew enough, he found out enough to realise that if he married her it would be in Mrs Westover's interest to claim that your mother had given her the pictures. She wouldn't be able to denounce her niece's husband. He went

212

over to England and stole the pictures and he must have found some Horsts among them. Aren't there some Horsts among them? You've just been down in that basement, looking—haven't you?'

'I have. There are four Horsts.'

'There you are, then. A fortune.'

'Calm down, calm down, calm down,' the Professor begged her. 'You're over-excited. I've never seen you like this.'

'You've never seen me at all. Type this, type that, keep that Frenchman out of my way, make yourself at home in that cottage and don't complain about the absence of amenities, my mother's pictures have no value whatsoever, and now that that's cleared up, I can manage for myself, so goodbye, Miss or Mrs a-name-I-never-can-remember.'

She stopped, breathless. The Professor, munching toast, studied her gravely.

'When people get excited,' he said, 'they usually become inaccurate. When you say I've never seen you, you mean that I've never paid you the kind of attention a man would usually pay to a woman as attractive as yourself. But seen you? Yes, in my own way, I've seen you. I've made my own observations. I know that you move gracefully—and quietly. Most women clatter. You use your right forefinger for putting stray strands of hair behind your ears; the right ear I can understand, but why, I asked myself, why not the left forefinger for the left ear? You show the tip of your tongue when you're staring at something you've typed on your typewriter. Your eyes grow slightly darker when you're angry. I read this once in a book, and didn't believe it—but it's true; yours do. You laugh suddenly—you burst out laughing, rather like a child. You turn the handle of a door and then you let it go and you push the door open—curious. You don't sing, or bawl, in your bath; you hum softly. When you come in after a walk, you look very young—about twelve, pink-cheeked and untidy. You are, when you're not arguing, rather a quiet person. It was that I missed when you went away—listening for you. It was a pity you had so strong a prejudice against professors. I would have thought you would have been proud of your father and his work.'

'I had to pawn the furniture, piece by piece. It wasn't as if there wasn't money—there was, but he never realised it. It wasn't until he was dead that it came to light.'

'And came to the notice of James Tandy. How did he get to hear of it?'

'When my father died, an old, rusty lawyer came to see me, to tell me that there was some money. They'd written to my father about it, not once, but frequently. They'd had no reply. It wasn't exactly a fortune; it was three thousand pounds, but that represented a fortune to me. James Tandy worked in the lawyer's office. Perhaps, in a way, I'm responsible for his taking to crime. I was good-looking, and we fell in love, and I had three thousand pounds and he had a soul that yearned for beauty. He was an auctioneer's son; he had grown up on the fringe of lovely things—never owning them, but coming to appreciate their value. He loved pictures and glass and beautiful china. He loved old silver. Until he met me, he'd been content to window-gaze—but there was this three thousand pounds, and a girl who hadn't the vaguest idea how to hold on to it . . . He was fun to live with. He was surprised to know that I meant to divorce him. If I'd been older, less hurt, more experienced, I suppose I could have made something of him . . . something of our marriage. But the idea of having been married for my money was enough; I couldn't forget it and I couldn't forgive it. Perhaps, today, I could—but I don't think so.'

'I don't think Mr Donne would have been fun to live with,' the Professor observed. 'Did you have three thousand pounds to tempt him with?'

'I met his mother first. She came to my office—she wanted a temporary secretary; she was organising a pageant. She gave me tickets; I think she must have regretted it, because that was where I met Malcolm. She's a hard and a mean woman, but she was right to see that we weren't suited.'

'Did she say so?'

215

'Not in words. At least, not to me. What's the time?'

'One o'clock. You want me to go?'

'No. I want to get out—outside. Out of this flat.'

'There's a full moon. Have you ever walked beside the Seine in the moonlight?'

'No. Have you?'

'Not with you. Let's go.'

He waited while she put on a coat, put out the lights, found her key. They walked out into the street, their footsteps echoing on the cobbles, rousing Bijou and Zizi to frenzied yapping. Two lean cats scampered across from one side to the other, almost under their feet.

There were others walking by the river. It was cold; Lucille snuggled into her coat; the Professor put on his mackintosh. His eyes were on the reflections in the water; he looked placid and untroubled. She thought that he was almost unaware of her presence beside him, but when she dropped behind to put on a headscarf, he turned and put out a hand to draw her back to his side.

They crossed the Pont d'Iena. They stared up at the Eiffel Tower as though they had never seen it before. He told her its dimensions; they entered her mind and immediately passed out again, as they had done so many times before.

'Walking like this,' he observed, 'one sees so much more.'

She did not like to tell him that she was not

seeing very much of the passing scene. She was gazing at a mental picture of a house on a hill, with a cottage near by, and a windswept terrace; she was seeing the Professor in his study, among his papers.

'Is the house ready to be auctioned?' she asked.

'The house?'

'Your house. Hill House.'

'Perhaps,' he said, 'it won't be put up for auction. Perhaps it won't be sold, after all.'

'But you don't live in it.'

'I've been wondering whether perhaps I'd do just that: live in it.'

She turned to stare at him.

'But—'

'I had a dream once, but it didn't come to anything.'

'What was it?'

'When I was a young man, I dreamt of a clinic of my own. I thought that up there, in all the good, pure air, I could run a sort of nursing home. It didn't come to anything—but lately, I've wondered...'

'How lately?'

'Since meeting you. You're the first young person I ever saw in that house—do you realise that? My grandfather, my grandmother, my father, my mother—and a steadily-dwindling staff of servants, all aged, because it was too dull for the young. But working in an institution isn't as dull as working in a private house; staffing the place wouldn't be a problem. I've got the reputation; I've got the house—and I've got the money to put it in order and equip it.'

'And how would the patients get up there in order to consult you?'

'By means of a well-laid road. It was a good road once; it could be again. Fresh produce from the farm. All those rooms opened out and used. The terrace—or part of it—glassed in. There wouldn't be any lack of patients, and I know at least three doctors who would be glad to work under me. It would be a busy life, but I think you'd enjoy it. One could live apart, in the wing beyond the dining-room; children could make a noise there, and they'd have all that side of the grounds to run around in.' He glanced down at her. 'A good life, healing the sick. What do you think of the plan?'

There was a pause. He wanted her to say something—but she was reviewing his speech and finding it almost totally impersonal. She was certainly included in his plan for the future, but in what capacity, she felt that neither she nor anybody else could guess.

'Perhaps,' he suggested at last, his voice dull with disappointment, 'perhaps you're tired?'

'A little. Let's go back.'

He said nothing. They turned and retraced their steps. In silence, each deep in thought, they walked slowly back to Madame Camille's.

Lucille stopped.

218

'Goodnight,' she said.

'Feel better for the walk?'

'Yes, thank you.'

'When you're not tired, perhaps you'd give that scheme some thought.'

'I'll do that. But I think you—'

She stopped. The headlights of a car had cut the darkness of the street. Round the corner came Monsieur Reynaud's car. The Professor went forward; when it stopped, he opened the door of the driving seat.

'I didn't expect you so soon,' he told Monsieur Reynaud.

Monsieur Reynaud climbed slowly out and stood looking at him.

'But you expected me, hm?'

'Oh, certainly; yes.'

'So that was why you sent us off together?'

'I thought it might be a good idea. You were both, after all, interested in the same thing. You were—I felt—bound to come to a little arrangement.'

Monsieur Reynaud glanced at Lucille.

'You permit that we talk upstairs?' he asked.

She led them up to the flat.

'It's nearly three o'clock,' she pointed out.

'I am sorry. It is not my fault,' Monsieur Reynaud said. 'The Professor has been having a little joke with me.' He faced the Professor. 'Very well, Professor. Let me please say that I underestimated you. From the first, I underestimated you. But you win. Where are the pictures?'

'They are where Mr Tandy put them—down in Madame Camille's basement,' the Professor said in surprise.

'Yes, yes, yes. But where are the others?'

'You wanted my mother's pictures. You can have them; they're all down there, untouched.'

'And quite, quite worthless.'

'Haven't I told you so all along?'

'You have. And now could we cease to play games? Where are the other pictures? There should be four.'

'Ah, Mr Tandy counted them? He's quite right. There are four Anton Horsts. I studied them carefully and I cannot believe that anybody will hang them up in their drawing-rooms. Two thermometer charts, an avalanche—I think I'm right in saying it's an avalanche, but one can't be sure—and a fourth whose subject eludes me. Surely my mother showed them to you?'

Lucille, after a glance at the Frenchman's tired face, put a chair beside him. Bowing his thanks, he sat down.

'She brought them to show them to me,' he said slowly. 'But although I had heard of Anton Horst, I did not care for his work; like you, Professor, I did not believe that it would ever appeal to the discerning. I thought your mother charming—and kind, for she was anxious to help this young painter. But she was not the first lady to come like this and try to interest me in these paintings, or in those. These ladies, they sometimes liked the painting, sometimes the painter. In all cases, they pleaded with me to buy, to advance the career of this or that unknown. Your mother did not plead. She banged with her fist on my table. She shouted at me to tell me that she was offering a splendid chance to reap a great harvest. When I did not buy, she called me a lunatic. She said I was not a true expert. She said that I would live to regret.

'And I think that that is all that would interest you of my part of this story. The rest I learned tonight from my assistant.'

'How is his head?' enquired the Professor solicitously.

'His head will mend. You know, I think, most of what he told me—but I will be able, perhaps, to fill in some gaps. I myself had not the slightest idea that he could be involved in the disappearance of the pictures. Not until I saw Mrs Westover in Paris and asked her what I should have asked her the first time I met her: had she ever taken any pictures to a gallery, and if so, which one? When I heard that it was mine, I knew everything. When I knew that my assistant had rented a flat with a basement, when I realised that he had gone to England in rather a hurry and was expected back soon ... then all that was necessary was to get to the flat, the basement, and ... well, you know the rest.'

'Why don't you make him a partner?' the

Professor asked.

There was a long, tense silence. At last Monsieur Reynaud spoke in a stupefied voice.

'Perhaps I did not hear properly what you said. Are you...'

'I'm proposing that you should raise him from assistant to partner.'

'James *Tandy*?'

'Yes. State your objections.'

'State my ... state my ... Why, the man is a thief! He is a villain! He stole pictures. He stole money. He stole some china—this he told me himself. He took the china because he was going to buy from Mrs Westover—from Miss Westover—the Horst picture. He was going to find a "private" buyer—but the private buyer must, of course, pay. And so to pay for pictures which he had not as yet stolen, he stole the china belonging to a lady who once had been engaged to marry him, knowing that she could not tell the police of the loss.'

'Anything else?'

'You think that is not enough?'

'Have you ever heard that the devil you know is better than the devil you don't?'

'For an assistant, for a partner, must I have a devil at all?'

'You know Tandy is clever. You know he's astute. You know he's a good judge, not only of painting, but of other forms of art as well. He tried to pull off a deal while you were away. He didn't succeed. If you get rid of him, if you expose him, what happens? You lose a valuable man, a charming girl—Miss Westover—loses a potentially good husband ... and you lose all chance of putting your hand on those Horsts. Because I intend to give them as a wedding present to Miss Carol Westover. I am going to a lawyer named—I think—François Ducros ... is that his name?'

'Yes,' said Lucille.

'I shall have the thing done properly—drawn up and signed and so on—put into her name and tied up nicely so that she knows what happens to them, if anything happens to them. Tandy's trouble, as I see it, has been in trying to fix the balance between recognising lovely things and owning lovely things. In your hands, he'll be able to indulge his craving for genuine works of art. He will have a capital—I've no doubt he will persuade his wife to sell you a Horst or two. You were going to buy all my mother's pictures—*en bloc*—in the hope of finding a Horst or two among them. You and Mr Tandy have a good deal in common. Keep him, use him; you were born to be partners. Your only danger will lie in my mother's pictures. Many of them, as you'll know, were painted under the Horst influence. The initials are the same: A. H. The themes are much the same. A little artistic touching-up here and there ... as I say, you must watch Mr Tandy. But I think that with a charming wife, with a prosperous partner, with an assured future, Mr

Tandy will be worth much to you. How about it, Monsieur Reynaud?'

Monsieur Reynaud was silent for so long that Lucille thought he must have died of shock. Studying him, however, she saw only a thoughtful frown upon his brow.

'I don't want to hurry you,' she said, 'but could you take the problem home with you and study it there?'

Like a man in a dream, he levered himself out of the chair. He gazed from her to the Professor, and back again.

'A good idea, no?' the Professor said encouragingly. 'I'll come down with you; perhaps you'd be kind enough to drop me at my hotel.'

Monsieur Reynaud bowed over Lucille's hand.

'I endorse part of what the Professor said,' she told him. 'Mr Tandy will be a good partner. I was married to him, so I can speak with knowledge. All you'll have to do is keep an eye on him. Goodnight.'

Monsieur Reynaud opened his mouth to speak, and closed it without saying anything. The Professor took his arm.

'Come along,' he said kindly. 'You're tired. You've had a big day.'

He led him away.

CHAPTER TEN

In the morning, Lucille made herself some coffee, carried it into the drawing-room and sat down at her aunt's desk to write a letter to Malcolm Donne.

She found it a difficult task—not because she was in any doubt of what she was going to say, and not because she imagined that what she was going to say would give him pain; he would probably, she thought, feel as relieved as herself. Her difficulty arose from the fact that events seemed to have carried her so far from him that she found it almost impossible to see him clearly. He was part of a past that seemed like another life—that was another life.

She wrote and addressed the letter with a sense of finality. All doubts were settled. It was a pity that he had come to Paris; it had been an atmosphere foreign in more senses than one, and it was her fault that he had proved so inadequate. All the same, she mused, getting up and closing the desk, it was extraordinary that a man who in his own set, against his own background, appeared to such advantage, should have made so little impression elsewhere.

Monday. A free day. Saturday had been only the day before yesterday, but it felt like last year.

Diana Bannerman arrived just as the flat had been cleaned and tidied. She was holding so gigantic a bunch of roses that it was difficult to get upstairs.

'From François, with love,' she said, dropping them on to the kitchen table. 'And from myself, with thanks.'

'I didn't do anything.'

'No?' Diana lit a cigarette. 'You bolstered up my courage at a moment when it was oozing out of me. You can laugh if you like, but that night, when François came here to give you those papers of your aunt's, I was screwing myself up to tell him it wouldn't work. I'd had too much fish-eye treatment from his relations. It got between the chinks of my self-esteem. I don't like to feel I overrate myself, but nobody's ever peered at me with that well-well-what-a-mess expression before, and I hope nobody'll ever do it again. It makes your self-confidence sag. I wanted to get back to where I belonged. So thanks. It wasn't so much what you said, as you yourself; you've got a calming effect—d'you know that?'

Lucille, assembling vases and beginning to arrange the flowers, nodded towards the drawing-room.

'There's a letter in there addressed to Malcolm Donne. I didn't have a calming effect on him.'

Diana frowned.

'You've written to him?'

'Yes.'

'Not to make it up, I hope?'

'No. Just to say I'm sorry.'

'But you're not sorry—are you?'

'I'm sorry for him. He lost some of his dignity here, and his dignity means a lot to him.'

'It's all he's got. I wish I could be sure you wouldn't let him talk you into giving it another go. In his way, he's not bad-looking, and once you got back to England and saw him against that good old hunting back-cloth, you might succumb. A lot of women would like that kind of life: stirrup cups and posing for photographs behind a lot of poor dead birds, and giving parties for Hunt balls. You get your picture in the glossies and you feel you're really there, but it all gives me the creeps, and it would you too, after a while. You keep out of it. You find yourself a present-day product. What I like about François is that he's free of all that weight of ancestors with long curls. I don't know how he shook it off, but he did. They talk to him about tradition; he picks out what he wants and lets the rest go. I wish you could find a man like him. Or perhaps. I mean I wish you could find a man and fall really in love with him. Love. Not that wishy-washy feeling you had for Donne. You want to marry and settle down, don't you?'

'Yes.'

'Then there's nothing to stop you. You're a

beauty—I suppose you know? You don't behave as if you knew. On one side of you there's this Donne and on the other the Professor—not that I'm considering him as marriageable; I'm just mentioning him because he's there. A woman like you should have, could have, a string of screamingly eligible suitors. Leave those flowers alone and let me give you some advice: fall in love.'

Lucille stepped back to study a flower arrangement.

'I have,' she said.

'Find some nice man and ... What did you say?'

'I said I'd fallen in love.'

'Ah, so *that's* why you couldn't bring yourself to ... But if you'd fallen in love, why did you let that Donne come over here?'

'I didn't know, then.'

'And here I was spouting advice. What's he like?'

'There's not much point in telling you; it's not fixed up yet.'

'What's not fixed up?'

'Well, I know I'm in love. I don't know about him.'

'You mean,' Diana said in a high voice, 'you've gone and fallen in love with somebody and you can't even ... Look, stop doing those flowers and let's have some nice, strong coffee.'

Lucille put coffee on the stove, finished her work and carried the vases into the drawing-room.

'Lovely,' she said, looking round her with satisfaction.

'Bridal,' Diana said. 'Now pour out that coffee and tell me about this man. This moron. Because what man could hold out if you wanted to ... Oh well, some men, I grant you. Men like this Professor, for example. You could let him loose among a hundred houris and his pulse wouldn't even quicken. But I'm not talking about borderline cases like him; I'm discussing real men.'

'Real men, as you call them, don't present any problem. It's men like the Professor who—'

'Well, yes. But let's just discuss possibilities.'

'I thought we were discussing love.'

'So we were, until you, or was it I, dragged in this Professor. Why not stick to the point?'

'He's the point.'

'Why not just tell me right out who...'

Diana's voice trailed away. Her mouth open, she stared speechlessly at Lucille. The cup rattled on the saucer, and she looked round, dazed, for something on which to put them.

'Come on,' Lucille said encouragingly. 'I'm waiting for this advice.'

'You...' Diana brought out at last. 'You ... and the Professor!'

'So far, only me,' corrected Lucille.

'I don't understand.'

'You should. Didn't you just say you could leave him surrounded by houris?'

'You're not trying to tell me that … that you've fallen in love with him and you don't even know…'

'That's it. I don't even know.'

'Look, are you serious? Is this a joke, or something?'

'It isn't a joke, and I'm serious. I'm in love. I ought to know the symptoms; I've had them before. I'm in love.'

'Since when? For heaven's sake, since when?'

'Since when?' Lucille repeated the words dreamily. 'I can't tell you, because I don't know. Since a long time, I think. When I first saw him, I thought just what you're thinking. I thought I could just bear to work for him for two or three weeks, and then forget him. The odd part is that I only took the job because I had lost my nerve about marrying Malcolm. There was this house stuck up on a hill, practically impossible to get at, and no phone. It looked like a ready-made retreat. I wanted to get away for a while—and I did. Today, everything that ever happened to me before I met the Professor seems vague and unreal. Malcolm and the office began to mean less, and now they mean nothing at all.'

'Lucille, you're crazy! Can't you see? All you're suffering from is reaction. You've got rid of Donne, and that's left a vacuum and in drops the Professor. He's simply not husband material. He's not animal; he's vegetable and mineral. Don't sit there looking rapt—come out and take a good, long look at the man. You could prop him up in a field to scare the crows and nobody'd know the difference. If he ever noticed a woman, it would be between two study periods. Have sense, Lucille. Do you really want to point to that man, with his glasses on sideways and his nose like a pen-nib and his clothes in a mess—do you want to point to all that and say: This is my husband? Do you?'

'Yes.'

'You're sure you know what you're saying? You really love this man?'

'Yes. How does one set about getting his mind on to marriage?'

'How do I know? If you're in your right mind and if you really want him, you'll have to use force. Charm won't do it. Sex won't do it. He's oblivious. That only leaves a good hard dunk on the head, and when he wakes up, he's married.'

'Professors do marry; his father did, his grandfather did. It shows it can be done.'

'Can't I talk you out of it?'

'No.'

'Then I won't waste time trying. But how can I help you?'

'By thinking of some way I could drag in the subject of marriage.'

231

'But has he given any sign of ... well, of knowing you're around?'

'He outlined a plan for turning his house into a clinic.'

'When was this?'

'About half past two this morning.'

'You were with him at half past two this morning?'

'Yes. We were walking along looking at the river.'

'And he was talking about a clinic?'

'Yes. There were doctors and so on; somewhere, somehow I was to be there too. But he didn't specifically say so.'

'Would it help if I went round to his hotel and congratulated him?'

'I don't think so. I'd like the initiative to come from him. Where are you going?'

'To put the thing to François. It's too much for me.'

'You think François can do anything?'

'Somebody's got to. I want to see you settled before you're old and desiccated. I'll be back. Thanks for the coffee.'

'Thanks for the flowers.'

She was not sorry to be alone. She went out and posted her letter to Malcolm. She walked to the corner shop, went to the main entrance and stood looking at the iron grille; it was locked. She was still looking at it when the Professor stopped beside her.

'You look thoughtful,' he remarked.

'I was wondering when Monsieur Reynaud went back there.'

'Didn't you know he would? I think they went back together, he and Tandy.'

'But you'd been there first?'

'Of course. Like many cunning people, Reynaud doesn't give other people credit for even a modicum of intelligence. He thought that I would think that Tandy was trying to get into the basement. Tandy was in fact coming out, having put the pictures there. You knocked him unconscious before he had time to lock the door. Reynaud knew that, so he let me pick up the key and keep it. When I took out the Horst pictures, I left the door as I'd found it. If I hadn't, they would have broken in.'

'Did you take the pictures round to the hotel?'

He looked surprised.

'At that hour? To arrive with pictures? To walk through the streets carrying pictures?'

'Then where are they?'

'Must we talk in the street?'

They went up to her aunt's flat. He looked at the flowers with raised eyebrows.

'Mr Donne?'

'No. Diana and François. Where are the pictures?'

'With your friend Madame Baltard. She was being escorted to her door by a very agreeable gentleman. He helped me to carry the pictures

233

inside; they're in the work-room, with the laces and velvets and flowers destined to decorate Baltard hats. We had some cognac, she and her friend and I. She doesn't like your aunt. There's nothing like cognac for bringing out the truth. Nobody here, it appears, really likes your aunt. Did you know this?'

'I guessed it.'

'Would it be all right if I stayed and had some lunch here? Or would you like to go out? I've had a difficult morning at the hotel, helping your friend Miss Clitheroe to get herself off to England. She wanted to come round here and say goodbye, but there wasn't time. She offered me her address; I pointed out that I already had it. I must say I find it difficult to understand how Tandy, after having known you, could look twice at a woman like that. Not that I think he ever had anything like marriage in mind; having ascertained that he could put his hands on the china collection any time be wanted to, he must have put an end to the engagement. Will you put me in touch with this lawyer, Ducros?'

'Diana was here this morning. She'll be back.'

'I want to consult Ducros.'

'She wanted to consult him, too.'

There was a pause. He was standing by the window, his profile sharply outlined against the background of branches. He pushed his hands deep into his pockets; walking into the middle of the room, he stared at the carpet and then walked back again.

'Did you,' he asked, 'think about that proposition I made last night?'

'I didn't know you'd made a proposition. You talked about using the house as a clinic.'

'Did you think it a good idea?'

'If you want to do it, if you've always wanted to do it, of course it's a good idea.'

'I couldn't do it for some time; I'd have to rid myself of other commitments first. The house is full of stuff which would have to be gone through, sorted; I wondered if you could arrange to come back and look through it and decide how much should be kept and how much got rid of. Shutting it up for a time needn't be a difficulty; the people at the farm will always go up and keep it aired.'

'It seems an easy place to burgle. Someone got in, helped themselves to a lot of pictures and got away without being so much as noticed.'

'Things of value can be insured. Why don't you say whether you like the idea or not?'

'I'm not quite sure what the idea is.'

'Haven't I made myself clear yet? I want you to take on the house, fix it up, run it—don't you understand?'

'What would you say if I refused to take on the house?'

He walked over to stare out of the window. He spoke with his back to the room.

'Oh, I'd understand,' he said quietly. 'I should understand at once.' He turned to face her. 'And if you're afraid of being pestered, you needn't be; men like Donne might hang round waiting for a woman to make up her mind, but I don't think I'd care to. I know I've nothing to offer you in my own person. I'm not cut out to appeal to women. It didn't occur to me that I could even make a reasonable husband for any woman … until I met you. You showed me that you could take something—a cottage, for instance—and turn it into something else; something that suited you. You could make a job fit you. You might be able to take a somewhat unpromising man and make something out of him. I'm not good husband material. I can see now that my father wasn't. If my mother had been like you, she would have stayed with him and made a life with him—but she didn't. She went away and painted and drifted about interesting herself in strangers—and my father let her go. I don't think, if you took me on, you'd go away. I could trust you to do the thing properly.'

He stopped. The room was very quiet. Outside, there were only occasional footsteps; the coming-and-going that clattered on the cobbles every shopping day was today stilled.

Lucille broke the silence at last.

'What makes you think,' she asked, 'that a woman is more interested in houses than in men?'

236

He stared at her uncomprehendingly.

'I've just been trying to tell you—I know nothing about women.'

'You've made several long and pointless speeches about your own feelings. Could we now consider mine?' she asked.

'All I was doing was pointing out that I am aware of my own deficiencies.'

'You needn't have bothered; I've been aware of them for some time.'

'I know you have. That ought to have made it easier for me to approach you—but it didn't. It made it more difficult, because I couldn't hope to put the proposition to you in any acceptable form. I thought about it and then I came to the conclusion that the only means of reaching you was to outline my hopes for the future—to sketch for you a life with me, a life we could lead together in a house you'd seen, a house whose possibilities you knew something about. I'm aware that there are more conventional ways of dealing with this matter. I put it in the only way I knew. I thought ... well, I thought perhaps you'd help me...'

'You can't help people until you know their requirements. And you haven't answered my question: which would you say was more important: a house, or a man?'

'Well, some men. But the only women I've ever known have been the wives of colleagues. I haven't avoided women. I like men's society. I'm at home in the company of men. It never occurred to me that I might one day fall in love and want to marry. The thing took me by surprise. Until you left the house, I had no idea … as I said, it never occurred to me.'

'Didn't it occur to you that if it ever *did* occur to you, you'd have to find some way of conveying your feelings to the woman in question, and also some way of finding out what her feelings were?'

'I told you. I told you last night—I mean early this morning, walking by the Seine. I've told you again this morning. I can't make love to you. I can't mouth meaningless phrases. I can tell you about what I feel would be a reasonable, worthwhile future, and ask you to share it with me. Perhaps I ought to say this with shame, but I've never held a woman in my arms. I've never kissed a woman. I've never slept with a woman. I might—up to now— have agreed that this indicated some lack in me. Now I'm only too aware that all I lack is experience. Not feeling. No, not feeling.'

'Then would you be so kind as to express your feeling in the usual way? May I perhaps show you? You put your arms round me— good.'

He was holding her closely; it was the desperate clutch of someone afraid that she would slip away and be lost to him for ever.

'If you take me on,' he said, 'I'll do my best.'

'Never mind about that now. You haven't kissed me.'

It was some time before she could put her next question.

'There's just one other thing,' she told him. 'Have you heard the verb to love?'

'Don't you know by now?'

'Yes. But hearing it spoken out loud gives a woman confidence. So would you please say it?'

'I love you very deeply, but are you aware that the telephone has been ringing for some time?'

'Yes. But I didn't think it was safe to break off in the middle.'

She picked up the receiver and heard Diana's voice.

'Lucille? I'm with François. You know what? He says he's absolutely in favour. He says it'll work out magnificently. He says you're to go ahead with your Professor.'

'Thank you. Tell him I did. I have.'

'You don't mean he said something you could get hold of? François! François, come here! Lucille is it really on?'

'Yes. The Professor wants to consult François.'

'What—already? Isn't it a bit early to—'

'On business. He's going to give Carol Westover a wedding present.'

'*Wedding* present? You mean she's going to marry that—'

'James Tandy is going into partnership with a well-known picture dealer. The Professor wants to give his wife some pictures she can deal with.'

'*He* can deal with.'

'No. That *she* can deal with. That's why François has to fix it.'

'I think I see,' Diana said. 'All right; I'll bring him round. Oh—one thing: the sea-horse.'

'Sea-horse?'

'Don't start that again,' begged the Professor.

'The sea-horse is mine—you agree with that, don't you?' Diana asked.

'Of course.'

'But François says it'll be awkward for you if you don't produce it when your aunt gets back. So I'm having it copied. She won't know the difference ... until she tries to turn it into money. Good idea?'

'Very good idea. Thank you.'

'Don't thank me. Any good ideas which appear to emanate from me are merely being passed on from François. Well, goodbye for now. We'll be round.'

'Speaking of sea-horses,' the Professor said, when Lucille had put down the receiver, 'I suppose you could say that it was that sea-horse that made you telephone to get me over here. So we really owe Tandy a lot.'

'If it hadn't been the sea-horse,' Lucille told him, 'I would have thought of something else.'

240